NAKED MAGAZINE'S REAL STORIES

ENCOUNTERS AND ADVENTURES

NAKED MAGAZINE'S REAL STORIES

ENCOUNTERS AND ADVENTURES

A Collection of True Stories
From Our Naked Magazine Readers

FOURTH EDITION
VOLUMES 4.3-7.1

A Boner Book by
The Nazca Plains Corporation
Las Vegas, Nevada
2005

ISBN: 1-887895-42-6

Published by,

The Nazca Plains Corporation ®
4640 Paradise Rd, Suite 141
Las Vegas NV 89109-8000

© 2005 by The Nazca Plains Corporation. All rights reserved. No part of this work may be reproduced or utilized in any form or by any means, electronic or mechanical, including photocopying, microfilm, and recording, or by any information storage and retrieval system, without permission in writing from the publisher. Printed in the United States of America.

PUBLISHER'S NOTE
This is a work of fiction. Names, characters, places, and incidents either are the products of the writer's imagination or are used fictitiously, and any resemblance to actual persons, living or dead, business establishments, events or locales is entirely coincidental.

Editor, Blake Stevens
Art Direction, Robert Steele

For Our Naked Reader's

Introduction

Since the very first issue, the readers of Naked Magazine have sent in their Encounters and Adventures for publication in the magazine. We found some of these stories much too "hot" to publish, but we kept them in the back of the filing cabinet -- until now! We brought them out, dusted them off and here they are totally uncut in their original versions.

If they turn you on, titillate you own fantasies or even get you to take a pen in hand and write down your own experiences, then we have accomplished our mission. We want to hear about your Encounters and Adventures so get them to us:

> The Editor
> Naked Magazine
> 4640 Paradise Rd, Suite 141
> Las Vgas, NV 89109-8000

Who knows? You might just find it published in Naked Magazine!

We hope you will enjoy these stories again if you first read them with Naked Magazine, and if you are a first time reader, then sit back and enjoy the most hilarious, craziest, and erotic true nudist stories ever!

Robert Steele, Publisher

Contents

===============

3	A Day at the Library
5	It Pays to have Insurance!
7	Subway Games
11	Mud Fight!
15	It's Only Natural
21	Walk in the Park
25	Late Night Dog Walk
27	Naked with My Straight Boss!
33	Hot Tub Graduation
39	Naked Jogging
43	Newman
47	Dressing Room Spin

49	Tom
55	Naked Submission at 41,000 feet
61	Naked Buddies: Trying It Out
65	On the Beach
69	One Passenger's Experience: Belize!
79	A Place in the Sun
81	Dames at Sea
83	High School Memories
87	Locker Room Huddle
94	Run For Your Life
101	Serial Display
105	Stripped Naked
107	What Will the Neighbors Think?
111	Beach Encounter
115	Naked Yard Hopping

117 The Ole' Swimmin' Hole

121 Oil On His Hands

125 Caught

131 Gratis Solarium

135 Gym Exposure

137 Total Exposure

NAKED MAGAZINE'S REAL STORIES

ENCOUNTERS AND ADVENTURES

A Collection of True Stories
From Our Naked Magazine Readers

FOURTH EDITION
VOLUMES 4.3-7.1

A Day at the Library

One sunny afternoon this past spring, I spent the morning rereading the ENCOUNTERS AND ADVENTURES section from past issues of NAKED MAGAZINE. I wanted nothing more than to spend the day roaming around somewhere naked, but I had a lot of errands that needed taking care of. One of those errands was a trip to the University Library. The South Bend extension of Indiana University is considered a "drive-in campus" so there isn't any on-campus housing. When classes end at the end of April, the campus almost seems deserted. This Sunday afternoon was no exception.

I got to the library about 1 p.m. and the place was almost empty. There were three employees working the checkout and reference desks, and maybe three or four students spread out among the first three floors. The section I needed was on the fifth floor. I took the stairs, checking out each floor as I wandered to see if anyone else was around. The fourth and fifth floors were completely unpopulated.

Four walls of windows surround each floor of the library. There are study areas in the middle, near the elevators, and windowed study rooms along the south side. There are large picture windows facing north and south, and the east and west ends of each floor are occupied by rows of shelves. The fifth floor is especially nice because there are huge skylights over the entire center area. There I was, standing by myself in a quiet, sun-filled area. Of course it got the best of me.

I made a complete circle around the floor to make sure that I was really alone, then I went back to a study desk in the furthest corner away from the stairs and elevator and took off all my clothes. I stood naked, looking through the rows of bookshelves toward the open concourse. I walked slowly from shelf to shelf, keeping a constant watch for any new arrivals. I lost my nerve once and ran back to my clothes, but didn't put them back on. I began walking along the outer wall again, stroking myself as I went. Then I decided to be brave and walk into the open area in the middle of the room. It felt great to have the sun shining down on me as I masturbated in what is normally a public and very clothed environment! Then I heard a sound; perhaps the elevator was on its way up! I made a mad dash back to my clothes. I was amazed at how quickly and quietly I had gotten back to my corner. I stood there; breathing heavily, my heart pounding in my chest, ready to grab my clothes for a quick dressing. But it had been a false alarm. There was no one there.

I was really feeling quite confident in my nakedness now; I walked over to the south, facing a picture window that overlooks the river. I stood there for all the world to see, cock in one hand, the other tickling my right nipple. But the world wasn't looking. The rest of the world had decided to spend its sunny Sunday afternoon anywhere else but near the library. I enjoyed having the space to myself, but it would also have been fun to have had the right person "catch" me at my escapade! I would have loved to have been spread out on one of those big wooden study tables with another hot, naked guy! Instead, I stood there stroking my own hard cock until I got off. Then I found the book I needed, got dressed, and left. Maybe next time I'll bring a friend!

AB, Mishawaka, IN

It Pays to have Insurance!

Two years ago, I received a letter in the mail pitching additional life insurance coverage. After reading the material, I filled out the card instructing a representative from their company to call me with more details.

Several weeks passed before I received a call. The agent said he'd be in my area the next day and asked if I could see him. I told him to come as early as possible, as I was leaving for vacation the next afternoon. We set up the appointment for 12:15 p.m., which gave me plenty of time to eat lunch and finish packing. I told the guy I'd leave my front door unlocked and to just come in and yell for me, since I'd probably be upstairs.

Around 11 a.m. the next morning, I unlocked my door and went upstairs to finish packing. Since I spend most of my time around the house in the nude, I felt I would have ample time to pack and eat lunch before showering and getting dressed.

I went downstairs to put my lunch in the oven and thought I heard the TV going. I went into the living room to turn the set off so I would hear the insurance guy arrive. I did not notice anyone in the room, until a voice behind me announced, "Are you the gentleman of the house?" I whipped around, scaring my guest as much as he had startled me (if I had been wearing clothing, I would have jumped right out of it!). The salesman was sitting in a chair across the room. He stood up and introduced himself, walking over to shake my hand. He apologized for coming early, one of his appointments had canceled.

Once introductions had been made, I apologized and told him I would have been dressed, had I known he was coming early. I started to excuse myself to go put on clothes, but he told me that he didn't mind me being naked if it didn't bother me.

So I sat on the sofa across from his chair and he asked if it would be okay to sit beside me so he could show me charts and other material. He moved to the sofa and started in on his sell, but I noticed him constantly watching my lap (and once he even dropped his pen to the floor in order to lean over my knee to pick it up!).

His obvious attention to my crotch quickly gave me an erection. I tried to hide it as best I could, which just made it worse. Out of the blue, he asked me if I knew anyone in the area who gave good massages. I told him I had previously worked in a health club and had given my share of rub-downs.

He asked if I wouldn't mind giving him a massage to help work out the tension he had in his back. I agreed, and before I could leave the room to get the towels and massage oil, he was already undressing. By the time I returned, he was nude and lying on my floor.

After the massage was over, instead of dressing, the salesman said he wanted to sit with me in the nude to explain the remainder of the policy. I agreed and got a chance to study the lean, young body I just had my hands on!

After the policy was explained to me, and having had the opportunity to give a nude massage to a great looking guy, it was almost impossible for me to tell him that I really didn't care to get additional insurance-so I wrote him a check for the first six month payment!

That was two years ago and my insurance man still makes regular calls. It pays to be insured!
RR, West Virginia

Subway Games

It was rush hour on a hot, sticky New York August day. Being in the subway waiting for the uptown local was not my idea of where I wanted to be, but I decided to make the best of it.

That is when I saw him. Typical construction worker outfit: the work boots, the slightly too short white T-shirt that didn't quite reach his pants, the well-worn jeans that were clearly used for heavy duty work. He was also beltless, and although I generally prefer tight jeans, his were loose enough to have slid down a bit to expose just the top part of the crack of his ass; not an unpleasant vision! He stood about 5-foot-l0 and looked to weigh in at about 170 pounds, about two inches shorter and 15 pounds lighter than myself. He was nice and beefy, but not yet gone to pot, as most construction workers seem to do by the time they reach 28. He was in his early twenties, so I guess he had a few good years left.

He was drinking a beer from a can in a paper bag and he looked just slightly buzzed. If I played my cards right, I could follow him on board when the train came and see if that ass felt as good as it looked.

As the local approached, he finished his beer and dumped his can in the trash. I followed him on like a shadow and let the crowd push my hand into the crack of his ass. It was nice and warm and we were packed together like sardines. No escape for this guy!

As we started to pull out of the station, he began to turn. This was no easy feat in a crowded subway car. I thought he would try to run away and ruin my fun as my hand lost its nesting place against his butt, and was left with nothing more than his side. But he kept turning and soon my hand was flush against his fly. I could feel the buttons of his 501s but, better still, something was stirring behind them. Not only was he not running away, he had obviously played this game before.

He ground his crotch into my hand as I felt him stiffen. He seemed pretty big, though I couldn't tell for sure, and I decided a different kind of fun was now in order. I slipped a finger between two buttons and happily it met flesh. No underwear to contend with. By the next stop I had all but the bottom and top buttons opened.

I maneuvered my crotch by his hand but he wasn't interested in reciprocity. He did give me his dick completely, though, grabbing the metal support rod above his head with both hands and closed eyes.

I popped open the bottom button for better access to the seven plus turgid inches of cock he was sporting. By now we were at 18th Street, which left only two stops before the train would empty out at Penn Station.

He was dripping heavily now. I could have easily pulled his dick out of his pants, but I would have much preferred to have him shoot in his pants and wear his come the rest of his way home. Besides, I didn't want to mess up the subway, myself or the other passengers.

I increased the rhythm and a look of deeper satisfaction engulfed his face. That was all the acknowledgement I received. A look to himself and for himself. I don't even think he had looked to see who was doing him!

I was still trying to figure out if he could blast off by the time we hit Penn Station, when the commuters would get off and the train would thin out dramatically, effectively ending our adventure.

When we pulled into the final stop before Penn Station, it was then I realized that he was completely oblivious to where we were, and oblivious to me. I was doing all the work and he was completely self-absorbed, which was not really the kind of scene I'm into.

That's when I decided to initiate Plan B. I kept working his dick, but as we pulled into Penn Station, I pulled my hand out of his pants and popped his top button open as the subway doors opened. He still had both hands on the support rod as his pants hit the floor! I had stepped away by this point. His pants hitting the floor was like a wake-up call interrupting a great dream!

All of a sudden, he must have realized he was standing there, naked from his belly button to his socks, with a raging, dripping hard-on!

New York being New York, it seemed that not one of the commuters even noticed him in their rush to get off the subway, although some of the continuing passengers and a few new passengers seemed to do a double take as they first saw him, before proceeding to ignore him.

As for him, he was beet-faced as he struggled to quickly get his pants up and put his dick away without breaking it! His impressive, cut dick was dripping to the extent that a long stream of pre-come trailed from the tip of his cock to his shoes. And I was happy to have an unobstructed view of his rather fine ass as he was bending over to pull up his jeans.

Once he had put himself back together, he just turned and stared out the doors, which had by now closed. He disembarked the train at the next stop.

I don't know if he realized that I was the one he had been fooling around with or that I was even still on the train. I probably wouldn't have done what I did if he had been a little reciprocal or at least a little more appreciative.

JK, New York, NY

Mud Fight!

I've known Brian for about 3 years now. He's 19 years old and a good looking dude, but very shy. He's still a virgin and that makes him frustrated as hell. He's had a couple of girlfriends, but they've never worked out. About once a month Brian and I would get together and go fishing.

Last week, we got hold of a small boat and went to Mosquito Lagoon to fish for spotted sea trout. It's been called Mosquito Lagoon for a hundred years, but the Chamber of Commerce thought it gave the wrong image to the area so it changed the name to Indian River Lagoon. It's about ten miles to the south of me, just north of Cape Canaveral. It's a wide area of shallow, grassy flats, and the Intercoastal Waterway goes right through it.

We went out onto the flats and drifted, using live pig fish and shrimp for bait. There was a nice breeze-a perfect day to get an all-over tan, but unfortunately Brian was straight (and he thought I was, too) so I kept my shorts on. I already had plans to get his off later. We fished all morning, catching quite a few, but not many over the legal size.

When the fishing had died down, I suggested we go swimming, so we headed for the closest place. It was a mud bar with a small channel running by it, and it looked ideal. I knew he'd swim in his cut-offs, so I hopped out first and took the initiative. Acting like it was the most natural thing in the world (it is to me!), I slid off my shorts. I had my fingers crossed, hoping that he would follow my lead. He knew I was a nudist, and he'd come across my bare ass before, but this was the first time I had intentionally stripped in front of him. He was in a quandary. He wanted to keep his shorts on, but to be "macho" he would have to take them off. I had put him on the spot! Being "one of the guys" won out, and he peeled off the shorts. He was even more appealing nude, and the white skin that probably had never seen the sunshine was in stark contrast to his tanned body and only emphasized the area I'm sure he preferred to keep covered.

I didn't comment on any of this, just went on like this was the thing men do when they're alone out in the middle of nowhere. Heading toward the water, I took a ball of mud, tossed it at him, and watched it spatter on his chest. That was all it took to get a first class mud fight going! He quickly forgot his nakedness with all the mud flying back and forth. It was an even fight, and we were both covered with the sticky goo when I made a tactical error and turned my back on him. He took that opportunity to tackle me!

We rolled around in the mud, each trying to gain the advantage, but his youth and agility won out. He got my arms pinned and was straddling my waist, asking me if I was ready to surrender. Going unnoticed during all the excitement of rolling and grappling in the slippery mud, we had both become hard. Without realizing it, Brian was sitting on my erection. I could see his balls resting on the head of my dick while he stared me in the face and asked me to give up. His hard dick was coated with mud, but I didn't need to be an archeologist with a pick and shovel to appreciate what I was looking at. Covered with mud it appeared larger than life and was more than I expected to witness. Seeing him bare and erect after all these years only made me harder. He had the upper hand, but for all practical purposes I had won and was viewing my one-eyed trophy right in front of my face!

I told Brian, "You win!" and nodding toward his erection, asked, "What are you going to do now? Rape, pillage and plunder?" I emphasized the word "rape." That, plus noticing his erection for the first time and the realization that his asshole was resting on my hard cock, threw him for a complete loss. I took advantage of his moment of confusion and flipped him over. Now, I was sitting on his dick, and he was staring at mine. I told him that he had his chance, and now it was my turn to rape, pillage and plunder. I would have enjoyed going further, but it would have ruined our friendship. I asked him if he wanted to call it a draw, and he readily agreed. I helped him up, and as we headed toward the water, I laughed and told him that it looked kind of funny walking to the water with our boners pointing the way! He agreed, and together with our erections, we dove into the water.

We alternately played in the water and sat or laid on the mud for the rest of the afternoon, having a great time. Naively, he even apologized for getting hard. I told him not to worry about it, to start worrying when he couldn't. I also advised him to put sunscreen on the head of his dick because it would hurt like hell if it got sunburned. Getting ready to go, I had one last grope. We had to wash the mud off each other's backs, and I made the most of getting him clean and admiring his cute butt. He had a tuft of black curly hair at the small of his back that trailed down his butt crack. When I finished cleaning him off, I slipped my hand down the crack of his ass, following that black hairy trail, and goosed his virgin hole. You should have seen him jump! I caught him totally by surprise, and I swear I got my finger partway in!

We had to sit in the boat for about five minutes drying off before we got dressed, and I had a chance to look at him objectively. He had a slim, muscular build, and I liked what I saw. I felt sure we'd do this again. I was thinking maybe the next time I'd strip earlier and get him to tan his pale ass while we were fishing. I also knew wrestling in the mud and horsing around in the water was as close as I was going to get to Brian. It would be enough. He was a good friend, and I wanted to keep it that way. Except for being momentarily embarrassed by his hard-on, he had a great time. I can hardly wait until our next fishing trip!

Brian's a nice guy, and I don't want to mess him up, but he took to skinny-dipping like a pro and really enjoyed it. I might not be able to turn him gay (and wouldn't want to), but I can get him to enjoy nudity and help him become more self-confident. Some girl is going to be very lucky someday.

Frank B., Edgewater, FL

It's Only Natural

With the back of my tanned right hand and forearm, I pushed aside the bamboo curtain and stepped into the sultry afternoon humidity of Mazo Beach. The buzz of hungry mosquitoes and the harsh caw of a crow shattered the smothering silence. Faintly I could hear a car rattling on the rutted, gravel road that leads to this public naked Wisconsin place. Like an oncoming train the clatter of loose fenders banging grew louder and louder. Abruptly the awful intrusion stopped. Silence returned.

The sand that mounded up around my feet was invitingly warm. Ten yards from the end of my toes, the Wisconsin River slid silently by. The water moved with a muffled whisper and an occasional soft pop or gurgle. The river's slipping past did not disturb the glassy surface mirroring the upside down bluffs covered with lush, leafy trees on the other side. The billowing, boiling curnmulous clouds made a motion picture with no sound. The air moved just enough to deter the insects and keep the perspiration that was lingering just below the surface of my skin from escaping. My eyes followed the shoreline until I focused on one man sprawled on a blanket.

Momentarily I thought of the 100 people who had been spread on this scorching sand yesterday. Today there were only two-him and I. The other people stayed away. I trudged ahead through the squishy sand, which seemed reluctant to release each foot when I tried to raise it. I walked toward the man.

It would have been easy to walk a comfortable distance down the beach to spread out my quilt far away from my beach mate. I didn't. Instead, I stopped close to him. I didn't speak. I just spread my tarp, then my quilt, and piled my towel next to my open low bottom beach chair. I shed all my clothes.

I spoke, "Do you think it's going to rain? This is a beautiful place; do you come here often? Do you mind if I keep my beer in your cooler?" He nodded and groaned but resisted my entry into his world. His posture suggested his reluctance, but my questions finally opened a dialogue.

His response gave me permission to look at his well-formed physique. His hair was full and richly brown. He hadn't shaved for a few days, and that gave him a rugged, handsome appeal. He had slender hips, and his upper body had been contoured by lifting something heavy. I guessed him to be 25 to 28 years old. He was completely tanned even under his deeply sculpted armpits. I had only been tanned like that once in my life.

I marveled at the speed with which he smoked Camel after Camel. Continuously he reached for one more can from the 12 pack of Busch beer he had brought with him. He puffed and swilled. The condition of his body was not in harmony with his habits.

"Is this your day off?" These words were the switch. Suddenly his words started to flow.

"I'm working the graveyard shift while the second assistant manager is on vacation...I don't see why they keep the store open. Almost no one shops at three in the morning...But someone would have to be there by four any way...I guess it really doesn't cost that much." He rolled from his position on his stomach to his left side. He propped his head on the palm of his left hand. "Four, that's when the dairy truck comes. It's first; then the produce truck comes, and then later the stock truck. Someone has to be there to let them in, I guess." He popped another beer and lit another cigarette.

"I want to be an assistant manager in dairy," he continued. "I want to do the ordering. Now all I do is work the order. I already make more money than the third assistant manager...I've been doing groceries since I was sixteen. I got my degree in agriculture retailing from UW-Madison last year. Now I'm working at Fontains in Madison. They have some great stores, and they are great people to work for."

The enthusiasm in his voice kept building. I noticed the wisp of brown hair on his forehead was slipping toward his eyes. At the exact moment the hair was going to cover his right eye, he whipped his head to the side and sent the hair back to its proper place. He had a black skin mark on his left collarbone, and he had a Band-aid on the ring finger of his left hand. I was probably looking too intently because he suddenly seemed finished talking. He abruptly took off his towel, walked toward the river, and slipped into the cool, dark liquid without looking around.

As I watched, his butt slipped below the mirrored surface of the water. I wondered why this handsome, obviously ambitious young guy with clear career aspirations was killing himself with cigarettes and alcohol. None of my business. I turned over on my blanket and focused on the sand that had crept onto the edge of my quilt.

A 1960s-ish couple walked onto the beach. It must have been their car I heard on the road. They moved close to my space. The guy had long, black greasy hair that fell to his shoulders. A dirty headband kept the greasy mop out of his face and off of his impossibly scratched glasses. The girl, who looked to be about eight months pregnant, was taller than the guy by three or four inches. Her straw-like mane fell mid-back on her worn cotton house dress, which was not designed for pregnancy. The buttons strained to keep the dress closed over her protruding belly.

"How long before the rain begins?" I said.

The greasy guy blurts out: "I seen that SOB swimming. Don't know his fuckin' name!" As he and the girl settled, he on a broken lawn chair and she on an overturned white plastic bucket, he told me: "They only let me work 4 hours today. They sent me home, Bastards! Not enough peas to pack, they said. So Sharon and I came down here. We just live a mile and a half from here." He keeps talking; I stop listening. Neither of them undress.

The UW-Madison man returns from the river. He stares at the couple as the water drips from his fingertips and his shriveled pink dick. He doesn't speak, but the local blurts out: "I come here often enough I don't have to take my fuckin' clothes off every time. Goddamit, get your nose our of your fuckin' magazine and get me a beer," he screeches at Sharon. She doesn't move. He gets ups to get one for himself. The raindrops are creeping across the surface of the glassy river. The upside down bluffs blur and disappear. Madison man quickly gathers up his blanket and starts toward the parking lot with his cooler and his empties. He pulls a blue tank top over his head and puts on high top black basketball shoes, leaving his ass exposed. He walks away, saying nothing as we watch quietly. All that remains is an irregular circle of cigarette butts.

The air is like coal dust. The rain suddenly reaches us, and starts gushing from the black clouds. Brian and Sharon huddle under their sleeping bag. I cover my towel, chair, book and quilt with the tarp and stand waiting out the deluge. Droplets of water run down my face. I childishly blow the water away from my lips. The raindrops continue to pelt my bare skin. In 15 minutes the quantity of water subsides. I retrieve my towel but never dry off. The air remains sultry and close. I take a step or two toward Brian and Sharon. This was the signal for Brian to begin telling me his life's story. I'm sure that Sharon had heard it so many times she didn't even look up from her magazine. Their ratty, stringy hair sticks to their faces. His shirt and her dress are glued to their shoulders.

He gets up, and we take a couple of steps toward the river. He tells me that he grew up poor on a dairy farm just west of Mazomanie, about 20 miles from where we are standing. He says he's been married before and has two boys, 14 and 16 years old, that live with him. He tells me he and Sharon have been married for a while. Whether he said that to legitimize her condition, I don't know.

He surprises me when he says: "Tonight's our first Lamaze class." I tried to hold my face muscles still so I didn't show my surprise. He keeps talking: "I love to pack corn, beans and peas ... you know it's too late for tomatoes ... but we really don't pack them anymore ... we just process, freeze and send everything to Big Rapids, MI. They package 'em...I love to eat fresh sweet corn. Pop it in the microwave for a couple of minutes ...I can't wait." His voice trails off as big rain drops splash into our faces. We quietly wait, but both of us know that the rain has taken up residence in this spot. They gather up their things, and no further words are spoken between us. Reluctantly I pick up my rain soaked, sand-covered tarp and other beach items. After a few steps I turn once more to experience the beauty of the beach. I start to walk out of nature's finest artistic accomplishments. The rain stops momentarily. The boiling, gray clouds open, and the sun sends laser beams onto the rugged bluff and still water. I wish I had reached out to the UW-Madison man. I smile thinking about Brian and Sharon as I hear the distant roar of their car.

Some naked encounters reveal more than naked bodies.

At a place like Mazo, where public nudity on public land is lawful, I experienced more than physical sensuality. I return to this place repeatedly to be with the wide and wild assortment of gays and straights that come to be naked, most of the time.

Seth w., Oak Brook, IL

Walk in the Park

This happened a few years ago when I was a student at the University of Oregon in Eugene.

My college roommate, Keith, and I were walking through the park very late one evening along a wide paved bike path. It was a warm night with a light breeze blowing. We were talking and enjoying the nice evening even though it was about 11:30 p.m.

As we passed a park bench adjacent to a bike rack, I noticed a pair of shoes on the ground at one end. They looked like fairly nice, new sneakers. Then I noticed some neatly piled clothes near the shoes, sort of folded. We stopped, and I looked over what someone had left there: a pair of blue walking shorts, a pair of white socks, a folded T-shirt and, last of all, on the top- a pair of white jockey shorts! I wondered if some guy was having sex in the nearby bushes, but then I realized the clothing we saw was for one guy, not two.

We stood there silently for a few moments looking around. I couldn't see anybody and didn't hear anything except the water running in the river about 10 yards away and the muffled traffic noise beyond the park. Keith wondered if someone was skinny-dipping in the river, but there was no clear path down to the water at that point and no beach along the waterfront. If someone was skinny-dipping, they probably would have left their clothes closer to the place they were swimming. I told Keith I thought a naked man must be close by.

We decided to keep walking and left the clothes where we

found them. Farther along the path I suddenly noticed a shadowy figure in some trees, so I stopped. Keith stopped, too, wondering why. I pointed to the dark area in the trees and asked if he saw anything. We could see the shadowy figure of a person slowly walking around in the dimly lit grouping of trees. Keith didn't want to go in there, so we waited out on the bike path. Finally, out of the shadows emerged a well-built Caucasian man in his early 30s who was totally naked!

Keith and I were surprised. The man didn't appear threatening in any way, so we just stood there. Finally he said, "Hi." We said hello and Keith asked him if he was cold walking around naked like that. "Oh, no," he said. "It's a nice evening out, and I just felt like taking a walk through the park-naked!"

I asked him if he did this very often, and he said, "All the time." Bicyclists and joggers were rarely in the park at that hour. He said he didn't want to frighten or scare anyone but that he enjoyed being naked outside and loved to go for naked nighttime walks.

Keith seemed more surprised than I was and said, "But what if someone sees you?" The man just grinned and said, "I don't care if people see me.... It doesn't bother me that you guys are seeing me right now." It was clear that he was not only enjoying his naked walk, but also liked to show off his great body. I told him I thought he looked great and that it didn't bother me at all that he was walking around naked in the park. I thought it took a lot of guts to do what he was doing.

"Well, it's my favorite hobby," he said. He told us that he would usually hide in the trees or bushes if someone came along but that he loved to come out for them and "show off" if he felt it was safe.

Keith asked him if he had ever been arrested, and he said

no, but he admitted that it was always a possibility so he was always very careful. He also told us that he liked to jack off for people-if they were willing to watch. Sometimes he would come out in front of cars parked in the parking lot where couples sometimes went to talk or make out on pleasant nights. He mentioned two guys who were sitting in a car talking the previous night; he walked out and got a cheer from them so he jerked off all over their hood and windshield.

As he was telling us about these experiences, Keith and I just stood there surprised and amazed. The man played with himself and became fully erect. Every so often, he would stop and put his hands behind his back and stand there modeling his body, letting his dick stick straight out, then he'd start playing with it again.

He started walking toward a park bench and we naturally followed, watching his graceful moves. I had seen naked men in the showers at the gym and the pool, etc., and also pictures of naked men in magazines, but this man out walking in the park totally naked really had me surprised and excited. I told him I'd like to watch him jerk off, and Keith jabbed me lightly in the ribs. I told Keith I was really interested and would enjoy seeing it, so we watched as the guy climbed up on the park bench, spread his legs apart a little bit and began masturbating vigorously.

When he finished, he stepped down, grinning, and his cock began to soften. He said, "Well, guys, I'm going to continue my walk, have a nice evening." I told him I was glad we met him and hoped to run into him again. He said, "I'm down here often at night, so maybe you will."

A few weeks later I was talking to some friends at a party, and someone remarked that a few nights earlier they had been parked in the lot down at the park when a totally naked man rushed out in front of their car as their headlights shone right on him. They said they were shocked and drove off. I just grinned, knowing who the man probably was, and glad to know that he was still taking his late-night nude walks.

Roger S., Seattle, WA

Late Night Naked Dog Walk

Ever since I was sexually aware, from around age twelve, I've been attracted to the real pleasures of nakedness, both private and public. I matured young, and although I was just a boy inside, I was plainly a man outside, and a well endowed one at that.

When we lived in West L.A., I used to go out after my parents had gone to bed, wearing just a towel...just a towel until I got clear of the house, when I would shuck the towel and go for a nice long walk naked. This usually caused an instant erection, so jerking off under a palm tree was usually the climax (no pun intended) to my nighttime adventure.

My paper route was particularly early too, and I would often bike around the neighbor hood delivering my papers totally naked. I only got caught once, by another kid my age, who, when he saw me, stripped on the spot. Danny and I stayed friends for a very long time after that, with occasional groping sessions in the boys locker room after school.

Most recently, here in the supposedly uptight East, I've taken to the occasional late night naked dog walk. There's a park right out in front of the building I live in, and I'm the only one in my building awake at that time. All last summer, I made a regular habit of leaving my apartment wearing only flip-flops to take the dog out to the park or for a walk around the block. I don't bring any emergency clothes with me, since I feel that if you're going to be bold enough to go outside in the city naked, why be a chicken about it. In my very gay neighborhood, nothing much surprises anyone. I've been hooted at by the occasional driver and groped by a passer-by or two, but not much else.

The only really exciting and different thing that happened was one night when I was out walking Charlie, my yellow lab, across the street towards the park. All of a sudden, Charlie saw something flash by in the grass of the park. He began to chase whatever it was, jerked the leash out of my hand, and proceeded to run rapidly up the block. I chased after him, my cock flapping up and down as I ran. If I hadn't been so panicked about Charlie getting run over, I think I would have enjoyed the feel of my bouncing cock and the whoosh of the wind up against my chest and legs. Instead, having forgotten that it's impossible to run in flip-flops and not having thought quickly enough to discard them when I began running, I tripped as one flew off one of my forward moving feet. I ended up falling flat on the sidewalk. Fortunately, I wasn't hurt, and Charlie, hearing me yelp as I hit the ground, stopped at the end of the block and ran back. He was soon licking my face, and I rose up off the sidewalk and grabbed his leash.

What I hadn't realized, though, was that above me, in one of the high rise apartments at the end of the park, a late night party was just breaking up. A group of about five men were standing on the terrace watching the whole naked ridiculous chase. As I dusted myself off, they began to applaud, and one even turned, dropped his pants, and mooned me. At this, I also applauded, and then, as showily as I could manage under the circumstances, I made a grand bow, and led Charlie back toward my apartment.

Walking home, my cover having been blown and having just recovered from a rather embarrassing situation, I realized I had a full boner. I felt the most incredible and potent sexual, as well as psychological, charge I can imagine. I hope I never have to give up the thrill of being outside and naked. And with your magazine coming regularly, I'll be reminded that I don't.

Name withheld, Boston, MA

Naked with My Straight Boss!

My boss has always known that I'm a nudist. When he hired me, I had only worked a week before I had to take a week off to go on a nude cruise to the Caribbean Islands.

I work the night shift for him. Several times after work, he and I would go get something to eat, or have a few drinks. The area where I live and work is a dry county, no bars to go to, and since he has a wife and kids, we usually just grab a six-pack and find a place to hang out and talk.

After about three weeks of this I told him, because I wanted him to hear it from me and not someone else, that I have sex with men. He said he was okay with me being a nudist and with me being bisexual. That was really unexpected for the small town in Alabama where we are.

So we continued to have our drinks or grab bites to eat after work. He had a lot of questions about nudity. I belong to two local groups. He said he would join, but that his wife never would.

One night after work, as usual, Mike asked if I wanted to grab a few beers with him. Mike is cute as hell, and even though he's married, I never pass up the chance to hang out with him. There is always hope!

After about four beers, Mike said he had to go piss. He went to the trunk of the car, I thought to get some more drinks, but I saw he was taking off his clothes and locking them in the trunk! When he got back to the car, I convinced him that maybe we should keep his shorts up front with us just in case the police pulled us over.

I watched and wanted his naked body as he got out of the car again to fetch his shorts from the trunk. He didn't have an erection so his cute dick was still flopping around as he walked. He handed me his shorts, but before he let go of them he told me he had never done anything like this before and was a little embarrassed to be naked while I was still sitting there with my clothes on! Of course, I got naked quicker than you could spit! He watched me as I went to put my clothes in the trunk, except for my shorts, which I threw on the floor by his feet. (Mike drives a convertible, and we didn't want our shorts to just blowout!)

Alabama is full of dirt roads, back roads, and it seemed we were the only ones out riding the back roads at that time of night. Then he decided to drive into town. Fort Payne is a small town, and I have driven through it naked several times, even in broad daylight. My car isn't a convertible, though, and I was a little nervous about doing it. But this was my first time naked with Mike, and I didn't want him to get nervous, so I hid my anxiety. I had wanted to hang out naked with him for so long, I didn't care where he wanted to go or what he wanted to do, so long as I was with him.

We rode through town on the main street twice. The only people who noticed us were a couple of women in a pick-up truck who flashed their tits at us.

Mike did get an erection riding through town. I asked him if it was for me or was it just the thrill of being naked in public. He said sitting at a traffic light, naked in a convertible with the top down, was exciting, scary, a turn-on, dangerous and like having sex for the first time. I laughed and told him that I was glad to be "his first time" being naked.

After we realized there wasn't too much going on in town, we drove over to the town park. "How about a swim?" he asked. I was sober enough so we went into the park without getting dressed and jumped the fence to the pool. The pool closed at 10, but the park stays open all night.

Mike jumped in the water, and I quickly followed. He went under water, and then I felt his hands around my ankles. All at once, he yanked my ankles up out of the water and stood there holding my feet up to the stars while I sputtered around with my head under water. When he turned me loose to let me come up for air, just before I surfaced, I squatted in front of him. His naked dick was just inches from my face, but I figured it was too soon for me to make a move. Still, I had to get my revenge for him dunking me under. I reached between his legs and grabbed the back of his knees. When I pulled his knees toward me, his legs gave way, and he plunged under water as I came up for air.

When the water cleared from my eyes, I noticed this move had turned out better than I'd planned! His bare butt was out of the water and right in front of my face. As he dunked under, his back rubbed against my crotch. I held him there for a few seconds then pushed his knees away from me. I felt his head between my legs, then against my balls. He steadied himself by wrapping his arms around my legs. I knew my dick was hard, but he paid no attention to it as he stood up, balancing me on his shoulders.

We played around and wrestled in the water for a few more minutes, which got me up close and personal with all his naked treasures underwater. One such time I had put him up on my shoulders, and he dropped back in the water, motioning for me to be quiet. While he was up on my shoulders, he saw a police car pull up, and the cop get out and walk toward the pool. "My wife is going to divorce me for fucking sure!" he whispered.

Then we heard a voice from outside the pool gate. "Stay still, and be quiet!" Whoever it was outside the pool intercepted the officer before he made it within view of us, but they were still close enough that we could hear them talk.

The guy told the officer he plays basketball for a local junior college, but he has classes until nine, and the campus gym closes at ten, so he comes here to shoot a few baskets after hours. They only talked a few minutes when the officer turned and left.

When the guy came back, he introduced himself as Jason. We thanked him for getting rid of the police, and he in turn thanked us for letting him watch us play naked in the water. He said it was something he had always wanted to do but never got up enough nerve. Then he invited us to play a game of basketball with him. Since he had kept us from going to jail, how could we refuse him?

When he and his friend David saw two naked men walking into the park, they had interrupted their game to check out what was going on. Mike reminded Jason that we didn't have any shorts to play in. "That will make the game even sweeter!" Jason said, pulling off his own shorts and tossing them aside. David quickly followed and got naked also.

What a night this was turning out to be! First being naked with Mike and now playing naked basketball with two college studs. The gods were being good to me that night!

Since Mike and I are a little older than they were, Jason and I paired up against Mike and David. I believe we played about four games up to 21 points, but nobody was really keeping score. It was a thrill to be on the basketball court in the town park playing with three other nude men!

After basketball, we agreed to do it again sometime, and Mike and I walked back to his car. We didn't get dressed until we got back to the plant where we worked.

Before I got out of the car, Mike put his hand on my thigh and said, "Maybe sometime when your nudist group goes white-water rafting or camping for the weekend, I could go, too."

I will be sure and let him know when. If there isn't anything happening soon, I may even plan a special event myself. Maybe our naked basketball friends would want to go, too!

Marlon D., Collinsville, AL

Hot Tub Graduation

I am 22 years old and a brand spanking new college graduate. When I was thirteen, I started sleeping nude. At about that same time, I became a junior counselor at a Boy Scout summer camp in Missouri. I had a cabin mate, and so at first, I wore underwear to bed. I just couldn't sleep, though, so it wasn't long before I'd take them off once I crawled into bed.

Once a week, the all-male staff would get together for a midnight swim, an event totally sanctioned by the senior staff. In fact, many of them showed up for these stress relieving times. About an hour into the first of these pool parties, someone said the magic word, and the older staff members (the 16-22 year olds) started taking off their swim trunks. This was such an erotic charge for a boy who had not even admitted to himself that he was gay. The new staff members were told this was a longstanding tradition, and that we all had to swim and dive off the board naked. Well, hell, it didn't take me a long time to ditch my trunks. It did take me longer to jump off the diving board. This was the first real time I totally felt the wonders of being free and open in the outdoors, and I wanted to savor the warm breezes on my privates for as long as possible. These late-night naked swims happened several times over that summer and the next.

During my third and fourth summers, I moved cabins to one down near the pool and made it a nightly practice to shed my clothes, hop the fence, and swim by myself after the camp had gone to bed. Also because of where my cabin was located, I had to shower in the open air facilities. Man, there is nothing like showering beneath a wide sky with dark gray storm clouds approaching in the distance. I was around sixteen, and the tradition of the entire staff swimming naked had begun to disappear. Due to my status as a veteran, I pushed to keep the tradition going, but the diehards had all but disappeared. The summer I was seventeen, I started going back into the woods where I would spread a towel on the ground and strip down to nothing but bug repellent. At this time-relaxing naked under the trees, my hands clasped behind my head, unafraid of being caught-I felt as close to nature as I have ever felt. I became a true naturist. And before I returned to civilization, I'd spread my seed across the ground.

That Fall I went away to college. I found out what it was like to have a roommate-he was about the most boring and smelly man I have ever met. In the small town where the University of South Dakota is located, it's hard to find other gay men to have a good time with. I think I met about five the entire time before I graduated, none of whom I was attracted to.

The summer between my sophomore and junior year, however, I met several men with hot tubs in the bars that I would often frequent in my hometown. In fact, this became my pick up line at the bar: "Got a pool? Got a Hot tub? Let's go!" I called myself the hot tub slut. This was also the summer, so I got a membership at the Gold's Gym in town. Wow! A private sauna, steam room, and hot tub-I was in heaven. I spent more time back there with all those men than in the weight room working out. Only a few times did anything more than ethical happen, though. The summer before my senior year was right up there with my all time naturist moments. I spent it living with my sister in Dallas. She had a tall fence, and I was able to spend two months sunbathing naked in her back yard while everyone was at work. There was a lot of construction going on next door, but I didn't care. I walked past the wide-open windows daring the hardhats to watch me enjoy the marvels of being naked. About two weeks before I had to return to school in South Dakota, I heard about a lake near Dallas that was known as a gay nudist spot. I tracked it down and drove out to a remote area covered with brush and cedars near the lake. The temperature hovered around 100 degrees and sweat streamed down my body as I walked back into the woods. I stripped off my white t-shirt and stuck it into the backpack I was carrying, but as I got farther along the well-worn path, I decided, what the hell! I stripped off my blue jeans and briefs and tossed them over my shoulder.

After walking for about 20 minutes, I knew I'd found the right spot when I saw three men in their late 20s who were as naked as I was (although I was still wearing thick gray socks and my hiking boots). Two of the men were laying back on an old army surplus blanket talking to each other, and the third was watching them from a boulder about 50 feet away. And I could see why. The two on the blanket were really extraordinary looking. One had curly dark red hair, which fell onto his forehead and a patch of auburn fuzz sprouting up between his pecs. The other was a blonde with a clean body down to his yellow pubic hair. Both were in great shape and had well defined muscled bodies that made my temperature rise even higher. I walked over, and we small talked for a half an hour or so, me standing over them with the sun warming my back, before we all spread our seed upon the ground as the man sitting on the boulder watched. I returned one more time to stroll the wooded paths in the buff before I had to go back to South Dakota for my senior year. This time, however, I didn't see anyone around.

This brings me to the last event in my life that was remotely exciting naturalistically (except for the fact that I am naked while word processing this). Last Saturday, I graduated from the University of South Dakota. My family and I stayed in one of the college town's older motels that nonetheless has an indoor hot tub and swimming pool. I'd gone through the morning commencement ceremonies (as much as I'd have loved to receive my diploma naked under my cap and gown, I wore a suit) and had packed up my room to move back home. When I got back to the motel, my body was tired and sore and I felt especially somber-my entire life was ahead of me; I faced unemployment; and I was moving back home with my parents! With a little encouragement from my mother, I decided to go sit in the hot tub. I wore loose-fitting blue mesh workout shorts, but since the pool area was empty, after about ten minutes in the mediocre hot tub, I shed the shorts. The hot tub had a fifteen-minute warmer, but I had to get out of the water to turn it on. When I got back in and made myself comfortable, I closed my eyes and started to dose a bit. The bubbling water was not very hot so I didn't worry about the dangers of overheating.

But then I heard something, and when I opened my eyes, a very young, very attractive man stood in front of me. I immediately recognized him from some of my classes over the last few years. He asked me if I realized there was a closed circuit camera in the corner pointed at the hot tub. I glanced over, and, sure enough, a security camera was pointed directly at where I was sitting. I began to stutter, "I'm sorry," when he interrupted and said he'd seen me at graduation and recognized me when I first settled into the hot tub. He works at the motel's front desk, he said, but that this was the first time he'd seen anyone naked in the pool area. He also said that few people used the hot tub because the water wasn't particularly warm. I said, "You're right about that!" but at that moment it felt very warm. Then he asked me if I was gay. I couldn't believe it. In four years in that hell hole of a town I finally met a gay man I was attracted to the day before I was moving.

His name was Tim, and he told me that the owners of the hotel wouldn't be around so he'd turn off the camera. He was getting off work in 30 minutes and would put a "Broken" sign on the viewer in front. I didn't think much more about it after thanking him, but fifteen minutes later he showed up in baggy trunks with a towel swung over his shoulders. He stepped in the water and asked how I could stand the water so cool.

I explained to him how sore and worn out I was. Then he said he'd always wanted to do his, and, as I watched, he reached down and slipped out of his trunks and threw them onto the side. I was beginning to enjoy the hot tub more and more. He smiled and asked me if I still felt sore. When I nodded my head yes, he moved across the tub to me and began to rub my shoulders and back. After a while, I looked at my watch and realized I'd been in the tub about two hours. My hands were very wrinkled, and I knew it was time to go. I told Tim goodbye and thank you, that I was leaving the next morning.

And so here I am, back in Missouri, typing this, remembering the last nine years of my experiences with naturism, and wondering what the rest of my life will bring me. I hope the being above will give me a lover who is a naturist like I am, and I hope he comes soon. In the meantime, I've located a local group of gay nudists, and by the address, the club meets only about ten minutes from where I live.

Name withheld

Naked Jogging

Many years ago, I lived in a rural area north of Minneapolis. The large track of land nearby has since been developed as a subdivision, but at the time the brushy meadow served as a perfect natural jogging area. Most mornings I ran a trail I made through the brush wearing only a pair of ripped blue jean cut-offs, natural cotton socks, and running shoes. As I ran, the cut-offs tended to slide down on my hips, and I'd have to pull them up. But soon I found the sensation of the cut-offs sliding down on the sweat of my bare flesh so incredibly stimulating, I quit pulling them up and let them slide further and further down my hips until eventually I stopped running and let them fall. Then I stood there naked with everything hanging out, the cut-offs down around my ankles until I kicked them off and ran on, naked, carrying the cut-offs. My body felt wide open then, in a way I can't quite give words to but that let my mind open up as well. I felt ecstatic. A tingling warmth of incredible peace rose across my chest at the same time, making my chest hairs stand on end. I felt like my whole body was glowing, the first time I ran naked like that. Of course, had anyone come along, I wouldn't have had time to pull the cutoffs back on, and they would see the pink cheeks of my naked butt bouncing along. But when I thought of this, the rush of warmth on my chest just intensified.

After a few days running along with the denim cut-offs thrown over my shoulders, I remembered a scraggly old ash tree that grew near the trail. I trotted over to the tree and threw the cut-offs up as high as I could, giving no thought to how I would retrieve them. (Even now, just thinking about doing this and thinking about what would happen if some guy saw me jumping up to retrieve them gives me a hard on.)

So it was a blast to run along without my shorts, my balls rubbing against my thighs, my cock bouncing up and down, knowing that there was no way to cover up if I encountered anyone. After 15 to 20 minutes of naked running, I jogged back to the ash tree to jack off before contemplating how I could retrieve the cut-offs. Sometimes it was hard to grab hold of the denim, and I'd think that I might have to climb the tree or else jog home naked. My heart would then begin to rush pleasantly from adrenaline, but eventually I always got the cut-offs down by throwing limestone rocks to knock them from the branch or by knocking them off with a long, thin stick.

One time I jogged along a different trail, naked as usual and carrying my cut-offs, without any idea of where the trail led or who I might run into along the way. I loved the vulnerability of possibly running up on some other guy running naked on the trail, or someone hoeing or gardening in their yard or maybe peaking out a window of one of the cottages that I passed. I didn't see a soul along the way, and when the trail came out at a gravel road (after at least 25 minutes of my cock and balls hitting against my thigh), I stopped and slipped on my cut-offs before continuing.

My naked jogging continued even during the winter months when snow banks accumulated on the ground. I liked feeling the warm high of being naked outdoors at any time of the year. In fact, the only time I ever saw other people during my naked jogging was during the winter. As I jogged along holding my cut-offs in my right fist, I heard a jeep bouncing down the trail. I dove into the snow off to one side of the trail as the car with three blond guys in their early 20s reached me. They slowed, and one pushed open a window. "Pretty damned cold to be running with all that hanging out," the youngest-looking and best looking of the guys shouted out the window, and the three of them laughed. Unfortunately, they didn't stop the jeep completely and join me. It would be interesting to know what the three blondes would have done to me if they had. After they drove on, I climbed out of the snow bank and returned to my jogging with a layer of snow covering me until the warmth of my body caused it to melt.

S.C., Sr., Farmington Hills, MI

Newman

The seed was sown in 1970, at age 25, when I discarded my pajamas for good and started sleeping naked. I found an added blanket on freezing winter nights to be a lot warmer, not to mention cozier, than long sleeve woolen pajamas which scratched at my skin and wrinkled up around my knees. In the summer, I kept even cooler without the pressure of the waistband of my jockey shorts. Besides, I loved waking up in that half-sleep twilight before my dreams had completely ended, when my half-hard cock would feel extra sensitive from rubbing against the cotton sheets all night.

In 1978, I moved from my city condominium to a small cedar A-frame I built myself on 3 1/2 acres of semi-wooded land. I loved the solitude I found that spring as I built the house. I'd go out after work or on the weekends, strip down to thick cotton socks and work boots, get out my saws and hammer and nails, and be with myself as I constructed my solitary dream. I built the house, which sits 75 feet from a country road, so that its position is reversed; that is, the back faces the road and the high-windowed, open parched front faces east where it catches the morning sun and the view of a descending meadow. The view is no more, I'm afraid, because I let the greenery of whole property grow as it would, and a dense brush covered the meadow. I kept a 50 ft. X 50 ft. patch mowed which I use for picnics, but the rest has assumed a natural state of intense wilderness green and brown and piercing gray, and after 19 years looks like a wooded maze of haphazardly trampled trails.

I sleep in a loft overlooking all this and have to climb down stairs and cross the large living room to go to the bathroom. One rare Sunday morning in May 1991, while I was stumbling though the living room to return to the loft, I stepped onto the front porch to take in some terrific late spring morning air. I couldn't resist the urge to walk down the garden path," the trail that meanders through the middle of the property (I have them all named). My neighbors on both sides were not home, but even if they had been, they couldn't have seen me. I lingered at the lichen-layered frog pond for about an hour, then in the eerie locust grove with its big stump, and then through the caressing brown grain of the barely field, and experienced a brand new feeling of freedom and contentment. It was like nothing I have experienced in 44 years of life ... and it was a hoot!

My property abuts 60 acres of farmland planted with oats and feed corn and fall pumpkins, and 100 acres of undeveloped green-gray public woodlands and meadowlands which I like to explore every once in a while. I cover the acreage without taking any clothes so if someone surprises me, I'm busted. This really sharpens my senses. It's like my whole body; every inch of bare skin, feels alive, every pore breathes and rubs against the warm air, giving a kind of caress. My sense of daring is stimulated, too, and I sense my body build up within itself a wild manhood that calls to all intrusive eyes. Its funny though because I have to continue to wear shoes and socks-like Achilles because I am very tender footed.

Once on an early summer morning, I almost ran into two young male hikers. Fortunately I saw them before they saw me, and I hightailed it far enough away so that they wouldn't be able to see me. I squatted down in the high grass, the weeds scratching against my hips and calves. I don't think they saw me through the weeds as they hiked past, but I loved the sense of my skin completely feeling the warm moisture of the morning air, my balls and cock rubbing against the grainy weeds, gnats tickling against the hair of my calves and thighs, and the guys completely unaware that I was watching them. I felt like I was involved in some primal moment then, as if I were a wild new man stalking prey on the African veldt. I made a sort of whistling sound as they passed on the trail in the distance. They turned back towards where I was crouched, but they couldn't see me. The funny thing is that, if they had, I'd have had to run away, and they probably would have taken the retreating cheeks of my butt as the white tail of a fleeing antelope! What a trip!

D. E., Indiana, PA

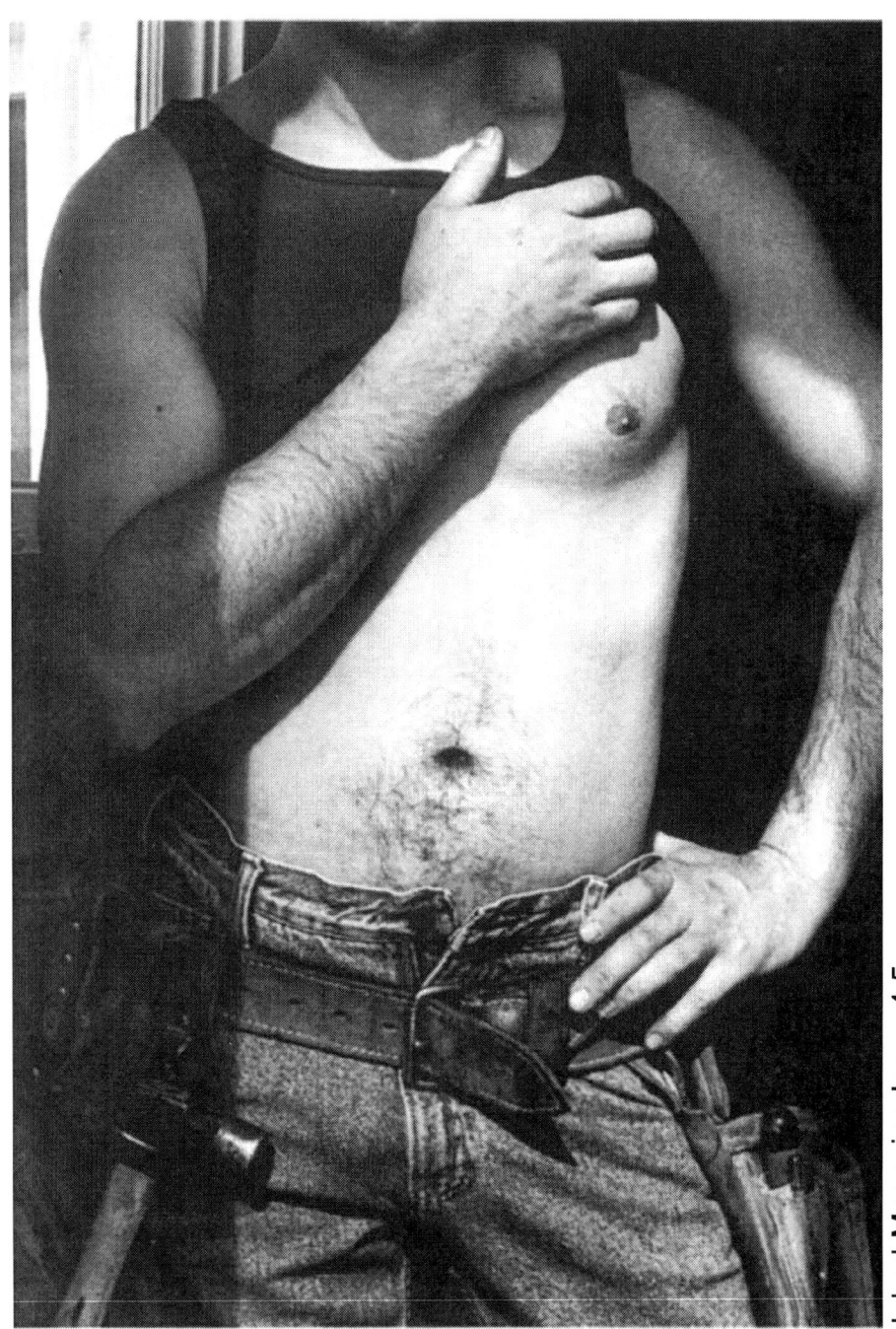

Dressing Room Spin

Several years ago my lover and I met another gay couple while staying at Timberfell, a very hospitable naturist resort for gay men in eastern Tennessee. Both are wonderful guys, and we became fast friends during the visit. Since we shared a love of spending naked times together, we have visited their home for weekend stays on two occasions. Both are very hot, handsome men, with clearly defined muscular bodies, and so the pleasure of their company on these visits intensified because they never wear clothes when they're at home.

Even so we do enjoy going out together. Last year during our visit, we drove to a local clothing store that caters to gay men. Immediately I scoped out the sale rack and picked up an armful of clothes to try on. In the incredibly spacious dressing room, my lover Todd and Cary, one of the couple, and I began undressing and camping playfully. Cary never wears underwear so when he pulled off his khaki shorts and tight black t-shirt, he stood there in gorgeous nakedness. We had convinced him to try on a funky outfit that consisted of a sheer nylon black top and trendy short kilt. While the gear did resemble a parochial school girl's plaid skirt and jersey, we can assure you that the resemblance stopped there. Cary, whose well-tanned muscles are exquisitely toned, looked spectacular. He seemed to enjoy the attention we payed him because we soon noticed the hem of the kilt starting to rise at a steady rate. Of course we told Cary that he needed to practice spinning around since he was considering the kilt outfit for his favorite dance club.

As he spun freely around, we caught several delightful glimpses of his long, thick, and luscious cock peering out from the hem of the skirt. I have never wished more that I had a video camera to record the moment. Cary decided that the expense of the outfit was not warranted by the amount of times he could wear it, so he returned the kilt to its rack. Unfortunately, all Todd and I have are our memories of his hot spin around the dressing room. Maybe we will return to the store when we re-visit the resort, and Cary and Aaron, next year. I'll bet we can find skimpy kilts for both of them since Aaron is every bit as hunky as his lover. Next year we'll squeeze him into "our" dressing room as well.

Name withheld

Tom

As a physician, I see lots of flesh but trust me; it's rarely the least bit erotic. Even when I have the opportunity to examine a hunky young man, the experience is usually clinical, rather than erotic. Exceptions are few.

The exception arrived in my office when I was practicing in a small college town. New to the community, I had established a contract with the student health service, providing additional coverage for their physicians. Entering my exam room, I found a muscular college jock-naked but for unusually skimpy briefs. I was surprised: my office staff knows that I usually meet new patients fully clothed; why was he undressed?

But I certainly enjoyed the view as I took his history. Muscular chest, nice biceps, flat abdomen, just the right amount of hair. His symptoms warranted examination. I palpated for enlarged lymph nodes in his neck and armpits, listened to his chest. I asked him to lie back enjoying the sound of the crinkling paper on the exam table and carefully felt his abdomen for an enlarged liver or spleen. Then I noted his shorts, now stretched by an obvious erection.

It was medically relevant to examine for enlarged lymph nodes in his groin, but I paused, realizing that this would require lowering his shorts, allowing his erection to be displayed. Would he be embarrassed?

Would I be embarrassed? I felt my own penis become stiff, and was concerned about whether I would be able to conceal my arousal. But my patient didn't seem to be the least bit apprehensive about an erection that he must have realized was at risk for exposure. I rationalized that it wouldn't be professional to perform an incomplete exam: "I need to check your groin for enlarged nodes." Without hesitation, he lifted his hips, and slipped his shorts down to mid-thigh, allowing his erection to flop against his abdomen. It was beautiful: huge penis, circumcised, thick shaft, full glans. I was shaking a bit (with excitement) as I carefully felt his groin and inner thighs for any enlarged nodes. I wasn't sure what was happening, except that I was aroused by my naked patient.

I wanted to retreat from the exam room, but my patient prevented this: "Doc, what are those white spots on my dick?" I explained that he should stand for that exam, and he bounded from the exam table, shucking his shorts off and tossing them aside. Sitting on my wheeled stool, his erection was now at my eye level. I carefully gloved and examined his genitals (there was absolutely nothing abnormal.) I asked him to show me the "white spots"; he pointed to imaginary spots on his shaft. I attempted to reassure my naked patient that I saw nothing wrong, but he had another concern: "Doc, sometimes I think I have a lump in my sac." Another detailed exam, this time unsuccessful, as his erection drew his testicles upward in his scrotum, preventing adequate examination. I pointed out to him that I couldn't adequately examine his testicles "while you're aroused," and suggested that he return later to complete the exam.

A week later, I found him on my schedule. I passed the morning distracted, wondering if the sexual exposure of my previous appointment would be repeated. When his appointment arrived, I knocked on the exam room door, then entered. This time he was stark naked. "Doc, I came back so you could check my sac for a lump ... this time I jacked off first, so I wouldn't get hard." I was surprised at the ease with which he notified me of his masturbation, and his apparent comfort with total nudity. This time he was flaccid, and I again asked him to stand, wheeling my stool around to check his genitals. Deliberately, I didn't glove, but instead caressed his sac, carefully palpating each testicle completely, with my bare hands. I realized that I was probably violating some oath I took in medical school, but enjoyed the experience. So did he: his penis began to swell and stiffen. I asked him if he had noticed any more "white spots," and he said that he thought he had, from time to time. I stroked my fingers up the shaft of his penis, then gripped his glans, inspecting it with my bare fingers, while my patient became completely hard. I told him that I couldn't find anything wrong, but invited him to come back if he had any additional "concerns."

I wasn't sure what was happening. I was just coming to terms with my own homosexuality, and wasn't at all dealing with my exhibitionist/voyeur bent but clearly recognized that we both were enjoying our appointments together. I repressed consideration of any ethical lapses, pretending my patient was responsible for all of the exam room behavior. But I wasn't displeased when I found his name on my schedule a week later, for a "sore throat." My nurses wouldn't ask such a patient to undress, but I wasn't very surprised to find him totally naked when I entered the room. His throat was fine. As we talked about symptomatic treatment, my eyes were drawn to his penis, now clearly swollen. He complained of "a little soreness in the belly," and when he lay down for my abdominal exam, his penis flopped upward against his abdomen, turgid. As I carefully palpated his soft abdomen, he became fully erect. (I allowed my fingers to brush against it, as my own penis strained against my slacks.)

The pattern continued, but the intervals between the appointments he scheduled became shorter and shorter. When I entered the exam room for the next visit, he was naked and already turgid: "Doc, I've got this pain in my prostrate." He became hard with my rectal exam, and I noticed a glistening drop at the end of his urethra after a prostrate massage. Prostrate complaints became his specialty. He reported dramatic improvement in his prostrate complaints with massage, and returned frequently for treatment of "relapses." Total nudity and a complete hard-on became the routine display upon my entry into the exam room.

With the warmth of spring, I noticed his body becoming tan, without a clue of a tan line. I asked him about where he got his tan, and learned of "an area by the river outside of town" where "guys can show it all." As the spring wore on, I noticed other changes as well. More bulk to his muscles ("Doc, I've been working out regularly.") I didn't comment when I noticed his pubic hair trimmed short, and the next visit, it seemed shorter still. At the next visit his genitals were completely shaved of every bit of hair, and he volunteered "I think it shows off my 'essentials' better." He spoke of leaving the university after graduating at the end of the term. I was frankly upset when I realized an erotic portion of my life would be leaving me.

Shortly before graduation, however, he called me on my private line. "Doc, I'd like to see you one more time before I go, but I'm up most of graduation week... are you ever in your office on Saturday?" Indeed, I could arrange to be--and I agreed to meet him on the Saturday afternoon after graduation. I explained that the building would be largely empty, but I'd leave the staff entrance unlocked; I'd leave my waiting room door unlocked for him as well.

I was alone in my private office, when I heard the waiting room door open and close. I went out to greet him. I wasn't surprised that he was completely nude but was amazed that there were no clothes in sight (had he entered the building nude?) And he was already completely erect (had he jacked himself in the hall, or was this a spontaneous erection caused by his nudity?) but as usual, he seemed oblivious to both his nudity and his arousal: "Doc, thanks for taking time to see me on your day off." I guided him through my empty office. "Let's check you over thoroughly, since this is your last visit here." He was certainly agreeable. And I had plans. I knew that I had long before crossed the line of appropriate professional behavior, and saw little reason to let professional ethics interfere that day.

I weighed him naked on the scale in the hall, and measured his height too. I measured his chest, waist, and hips. I teased him, suggesting that "most guys want to know how they compare in another dimension," and he expressed interest that I interpreted as permission to measure his erection. As he stood in the hall, I suggested that he stroke himself to get accurate measurements, and pretended that genital assessment was a science that required multiple measurements of circumference. I guided him to the business office: "Let's make sure I've got your forwarding address correct." We moved to the exam room for a detailed exam of his chest, arms, legs, abdomen, and groin. "Sexually transmitted diseases are common among students; do you have any problems?"

"Doc, I don't think so, but check me out." I examined his erection for any sign of herpes (there were none.) I discussed the risk of testicular cancer in young men, and suggested an ultrasound examination (I had just gotten the portable ultrasound equipment.) I oiled his shaved scrotum, and studied his testicles carefully, revealing their normalcy. I told him that prostrate disease was unusual in a man his age, but that I'd be happy to screen him for prostatic enlargement without charge. The lubricated ultrasound probe went up his rectum, and I did an unusually detailed ultrasound exam. Then, a digital exam, my gloved finger massaging his prostrate. "Doc, is it unusual for me to get a discharge when you do all of this?"

I suggested that the penile discharge be examined to determine its origin, and made a smear on a microscope slide. We looked at it together under the two-headed microscope, seeing motile sperm on the slide, but no white cells. "Looks like a healthy discharge from your seminal vesicles-some guys 'leak' before orgasm." I suggested an extensive prostrate massage "to try to get you through the summer." We returned to the exam room. I put his legs in the stirrups and began to manipulate his anus and massage his prostrate, watching my patient as he became flushed and began to squirm with obvious sexual arousal.

I told him that ejaculation was nature's way of "cleaning the pipes", and that the debris we were "shaking loose" didn't belong in his prostrate. He seemed to understand that I was giving him permission to masturbate. He began to stroke his penis, as I continued my internal massage. It didn't take long for him to ejaculate onto his chest and abdomen.

He accepted my offer of tissues to wipe off his semen. He wasn't the least bit embarrassed when he left the exam room still with an erection, still with a sexual flush. He thanked me for the care that I had given him, shook my hand, and left the office still stark naked, without any clothes. I returned to my office, immediately undressed, and masturbated.

I never saw him again. At that point in my life, I didn't understand his casual attitude towards nudity, or his absence of embarrassment at sexual displays. But that summer, I developed my all-over tan at the spot along the river that he mentioned during our visits. And nearly a decade later, I now understand my patient much better.

(Tom, if you're reading this, now I understand-and thanks!)

Doc

Naked Submission at 41,000 feet

It began as a simple transatlantic flight 12 and a half hours to Athens. Most of the general public are happy to simply board an aircraft, sit back, relax and enjoy the flight. Me, I have to make every flight an adventure.

My standard rigor is to fly economy and spend the whole time complaining about the bitchy stewardesses and the bad food. One faithful day, through no error on my part, I was upgraded to First Class and since that day, I've been a devotee. That's where my adventure into the secretly veiled world of gay male nudity begins.

As I walked down the gateway to the whale-like belly of the 747, I began to feel uncomfortable in my Donna Karen linen trousers and summer sweater (Well hey, if you're going to wear clothes, wear the best). One hand was holding a leather knapsack, which was growing increasingly tiresome, and the other was fiddling with my boarding pass. Finally, after what seemed an eternity, I reached the door where the flight crew were greeting the arriving passengers.

I can't remember exactly how he welcomed me aboard, but his name was Kristos. He was obviously Greek because of his accent, olive skin, dark, wavy hair; and although it was masked under a structured uniform, he had the muscled body of Zeus. Flashing his beautiful white teeth, Kristos smiled and informed me he would be my personal attendant in First Class this evening.

The flight began as 99 percent of flights do-grid locked

and late. It wasn't until about one hour into the flight when Kristos made his reappearance. It was also at this point I took notice of my surroundings. Instead of there being a full First Class section (other than the three people in the upstairs bubble), I was the only one present. Kristos came by with drink list in hand to ask what would quench my thirst.

Upon ordering a cranberry juice and vodka, Kristos made a compliment about the braided gold necklace I was wearing. "With a necklace like that, why would you need to wear anything else?" he asked. Then a very interesting thought popped into my head. What if half-way into the flight I didn't wear anything else. I then decided I would test my theory later.

After shedding 70 lbs. of excess weight over the last year, I looked and felt like a totally different person. When I was heavier, I was very cautious about taking off my clothes. Yes, I was ashamed of my body image and feeling how I could never live up to my expectations or the picky ones of the gay community. But that was before I started reading Naked Magazine. Now I will bare my new body at the first opportunity.

My improved body is sleek, with nice muscle definition. As soon as I began to lift weights and run, my body began to morph into a different shape. My once droopy chest is now muscled and defined; my stomach no longer protrudes, it just ripples; my once fat ass has now developed into a fairly nice bubble butt. Add some body piercings in my ear, navel and both nipples plus my mulatto features and the whole package is pretty hot and ready.

As we sped out over the Atlantic, the lights were turned down low and movies began playing throughout the aircraft. Many of the passengers took this as their cues to sleep, watch the movie, chat quietly or read. I viewed this as my opportunity to find out about the legendary "mile high club."

It took this gorgeous, humpy, hunk of Greek god about two minutes to return with my drink. As he handed it to me he asked if I wanted anything else before hors d'oeuvres were served. I off-handedly inquired if I was the only one in First Class for the next ten hours. Kristos informed me that the airline had strict regulations about the privacy of First Class passengers and he was the Senior Pursuer especially assigned to my section.

Devilish thoughts crossed my mind, and I simply asked him, "are you willing to go to any length to make me happy?"

A similar wicked grin came across his face when he replied, "yes." Even though the words 'lets get naked' were never said, there was a very heavy sexual tension in the cabin air. Kristos immediately lowered his lips to mine and kissed me so passionately I thought my already randy dick was going to rip through the linen of my pants. He then spun on his heels and let me know he would personally see to it we were not disturbed by anyone.

So here I am in a 747 flying across the Atlantic, hot, bothered, horny and ready to show off my nudist tendencies. I could hear my friends back home saying, "this would only happen to you."

Momentarily, I stepped into the bathroom to pee and I caught a glimpse of myself in the mirror. My eyes reflected the look of a panther about to mate. I did appear rather hot and horny but I didn't care, I wanted this man. As I returned to take my seat, I was stopped by Kristos who proceeded to french kiss me in the aisle. I pointed to the curtain separating our growing displays of passion from being witnessed by the rest of the aircraft. He whispered that he had taken care of everything.

I pushed this muscled Adonis away, sat very provocatively, and asked him to demonstrate his ability to attend to a First Class passenger. I told him to strip naked-no underwear or anything. So without further hesitation he began to reach for the buttons on his jacket. I just sat on the armrest, in total lust, watching, his jacket hit the carpet followed by airline-crested shirt and tie, the belt and finally, his pants.

When they hit the floor, he placed a very muscular leg in my lap and asked me to remove his shoes.

I can't remember if I was breathing or not. Of course, I was somewhat fearful of being seen by other passengers or crew and actually, I thought I was about to pass out from sexual lust. But my hand began to untie his dress shoes as a trickle of sweat ran down my neck. He balanced himself on my seat back, leaned over and licked it off just before it could disappear down my sweater.

This man was beautiful even with one shoe on. He had a finely developed chest, two huge nipples-both pierced, a defined waist, a stomach so flat and rippled it made me envious and the nicest 10-inch piece of uncut meat I had ever seen. After he was naked, Kristos decided, without any protest, to undress me himself. In about what seemed an eternity, I was free of the confines of my clothes.

Now I have experienced many wonderful sensations in my lifetime, but none were as erotic or stimulating as having fine champagne poured over my body and being licked off. For the next nine and a half hours, Kristos and I were completely naked. There were times when I thought some crewmember would show up and interrupt our experience, but Kristos had really taken care of things.

He was the most attentive, lusty and passionate man I had ever met. If this man was a dream, I didn't want to wake up.

He didn't leave my side for the entire time we were in the air. Kristos served me completely naked and catered to every sexual craving I had. He even satiated some I didn't even know I had.

As the captain announced we would be landing in Greece in 45 minutes, my heart began to sink. All this time, I was feeling like Prince Charming and now the clock was just about to strike midnight. Kristos told me as he was getting dressed and preparing to ready the cabin and crew for arrival, to not worry and that we would meet again.

At the time, the sound of a 747's wheels hitting the asphalt runway was the most unwelcome sound in the world. But it happened as we touched down on time in Greece. As I was about to gather my belongings and leave Kristos stopped me in my tracks, kissed and hugged me and whispered in my ear, "when you get into the airport, look in your bag."

Thinking that's it, he's a drug runner, I walked down the stairs into the hot Athens sun. Opening my bag, I found three things: Kristos' telephone numbers in Greece and North America, his flight wings and a note written on airline stationary. Then simply stated, "meet me by the baggage claim in 20 minutes. Don't leave without me."

As I walked towards the terminal, I thought to myself, I am dreaming. Sure enough, as I made it through customs and claimed my baggage, Kristos was standing there out of his uniform, shirtless and wearing shorts, a baseball cap, white socks and black army boots. I remember walking over to him and thinking that I was due in Mykonos that night for a party. Just as I opened my mouth to tell him I couldn't stay, he began to French kiss me again, much deeper than before.

The last thing I remember about my arrival in Athens is watching our cab leave the curb. As an Olympic Airways plane took off just over us, I stared at my Greek, nudist love god and said, "I think that's my connection to Mykonos." Kristos just smiled, removed my sweater, said, "I think you're right," and began to tongue my nipples again.

Conrad M., Canada

Naked Buddies: Trying It Out

I have known Eric just over ten years. Shortly after we met, he found out I was gay (he was too), that I liked going to the gym (again he did too), and that I am a nudist (an unusual concept for him at the time).

The way he found out about my nude activities was because of the gym. I'd always take my time while changing, never rushing like a lot of guys do. When I'd go to the steam room, I'd sit on my towel instead of wrapped around like a lot of other guys. Eventually Eric started doing the same around the gym, but I knew he should be enjoying it more.

Not only did Eric and I see each other at the gym and socially, we did conduct business together. Since I worked out of my home about 50% of the time and Eric about 25%, I figured that this might be the way to introduce him to more nude freedom.

That day came, and I told him that I would handle lunch, and would discuss business afterwards. The only thing that was happening with him was a call he had set up for about the same time. No problem, it was all working out wonderfully well. I arrived at his house a little bit before his call was due, with a pizza made and ready to bake (so he wouldn't have to worry about letting it get cold while on his call). I put it in the refrigerator and went out to his home office and in about 15 seconds I was naked with my clothes folded and in a corner. I went back to reading a magazine.

At the conclusion of his phone call he came through and

headed towards the kitchen and turned on the oven for the pizza and yelled back to see what I wanted to drink, I yelled back, somewhat surprised that he didn't at least pop his head in on his way to the kitchen. I got up and stood there waiting at the kitchen door. His back was turned but we were carrying on a conversation for what seemed to be an eternity. When he finally turned around, I was glad that he didn't have anything in his hand (or else we would have been cleaning up a mess). The smile on his face was so huge, it was like he was seeing me naked for the first time, but then again, it was not a new sight for him. We ate lunch at the kitchen table and then went to his office for business.

Even though Eric had seen me naked before, you could tell that this was a new experience for him. I knew that he was sorting through a lot of things in his mind so I never pushed him to remove any or all of his clothes. When we were finished and Eric was watching me get dressed to go, he did say that I really looked relaxed, free, and ready to conquer the world, and of course, I agreed.

We still went to the gym together and he did enjoy his nudity while there, however when it came to business or socialization, I was the naked one, and he was fully clothed regardless of the situation or whose house we were at.

About two months later, things began to change. I was working at home when the doorbell rang, and is my custom I grabbed my robe and answered the door. It was Eric, so off came the robe, wanting to discuss some business, but first he needed to use the bathroom, so I went back into my office. When I looked up, I saw Eric standing at my door completely naked. All I could do was get up and give him a great big bear hug. Eric told me that after the first time he saw me naked outside of the gym he envied the freedom that I had, and he started doing it by himself and found out the thrill. He wanted to get naked with me before this, but never could work up the courage until he told himself to just do it.

Now after many years, not only do Eric and I get together to conduct business in the nude, but on a social nature as well. Last week while we were hiking in the mountains we came across a mutual friend from the gym, Rick (fully clothed), on the trail. Rick was turning red faced and was stammering, but after he calmed down, he began to ask questions-lots and lots of questions. Even after our hike, Rick continued to ask Eric and myself about nudity.

Soon Rick, Eric or I will be ready to give you another adventure. I know Rick will be enjoying the thrill of complete freedom.

Glenn, Denver, Colorado

On the Beach

As a child, my parents had a difficult time keeping a swimsuit on me in the summer. In fact, our family often skinny-dipped together on camping trips. I was fascinated by sleeping nude, feeling the cold sheets against my skin.

As a teenager, I loved going for bike rides in the country, swimming nude in a gravel pit pond and sunbathing on its stony banks. Occasionally a friend and I would explore the woods near our homes, and each other, in the innocent play of teenage boys sans clothing.

I remember the adolescent excitement of finding my father's Playboy Magazine "Year in the Movies" issues, or old nudist magazines, that actually showed naked male bodies in all their glory. I've always enjoyed seeing naked men as much as being naked myself. In college there was great camaraderie in sunbathing nude on the fraternity house deck with gin and tonics in our hands, taking trips to the mountains for an all-over tanning on a snow bank, or late night trips to hot springs. Of course, I never let my fascination with the nude male body be known to anyone. I was far from being able to deal with my personal sexuality conflicts.

In later years, as I became more comfortable and honest with myself, I began to frequent nude beaches outside of Portland at Sauvie Island and Rooster Rock. There is something totally liberating about the sun, wind and water on a naked body in the peacefulness of the outdoors. The memorable fear I had of being around nude boys in the locker room as a kid and being found out or aroused disappears in the safety of a beautiful nude beach frequented by gay men totally at ease with themselves in the elements. My enjoyment of outdoor nudity has also taken me to incredible locations in Mexico, the Caribbean, Hawaii, British Columbia, Washington State, Florida, and California.

Two experiences at nude beaches are brilliant memories of the pleasure of being naked.

Several years ago I was sunbathing in a very isolated area of Sauvie Island when a fully clothed young man, carrying a backpack, walked up to me and nervously asked me if the beach was a "gay nude beach." I told him that it was, if the person who happened to be on the beach was gay. He explained that he had never been to a nude beach before, didn't know if he was in fact gay and never touched another man before. He then asked my permission to touch my body and without hesitation my permission was granted. Still fully clothed, he put down his backpack, straddled my nude body and proceeded to massage every inch of my sun-warmed skin. I was asked to roll over, and he did the same to the backside of my body, with a particularly great deal of attention to my ass cheeks and the crevice between them. Becoming fully aroused by this, I was somewhat embarrassed about turning over on my back, but I did so when he asked me to return to my original position. As he told me of never holding another man's hard-on, he wrapped his hand around mine and began a rhythmic stroke. He smiled down at me, while fondling my chest and playing with my nipples. In a short time, I came to a violent climax. My anonymous friend rubbed the warm liquid into my skin, reached for his backpack and stood up. As he started to walk away, he turned and said, "Thanks for answering my question."

My other most memorable adventure also involved an anonymous encounter. I arrived at the nude beach on Rooster Rock late in the afternoon, found a space protected from the breeze, and immediately fell asleep in the warm glow of the fall sunshine. A sudden lack of sun jolted me awake, and I squinted to take in the muscular physique of the male figure standing over me in shadow, blocking the warmth. All I could determine was the person had wind-blown blond hair, an incredible tan, and a great body. With the sun in my eyes, I couldn't see his face at all. He knelt down and began licking the inside of my thighs and beneath my balls. He took both of my balls into his mouth and worked them around until I could stand it no longer. I pushed his head off my crotch, but he made every effort to keep me from seeing his face. Then I felt the wetness of his mouth as he engulfed my cock and finished me off in a few brief moments. I was too stunned to even speak as he stood, still keeping his face from view, and walked away back down the beach, giving me a wonderful view of his bronzed bubble butt.

There have many other interesting experiences while nude in the great outdoors, but these two have always been exceptional memories. It is much more than the fact that they were totally anonymous encounters that turned sexual. There was tremendous sensuality, tenderness, and innocence in the encounters, highlighted by the warmth of the sun's rays, a breeze off the river, and the freedom of being naked outdoors.

Jeff F., Portland, Oregon

One Passenger's Experience: Belize!

When Roger and I received the info for the cruise among the islands of Honduras and Belize, there was no doubt that we would sign up. We had signed on to the first gay-nude cruise in the eastern Caribbean and the gay-nude cruise through the Greek Isles. We enjoyed both. Why would we not sign on for this one?

Roger looked forward to meeting with the friendly guys with whom we had cruised before and making friends with new guys. I looked forward to the same but also to the snorkeling. At that, Roger insisted that my son, Mark, also go to keep an eye on Dad. Mark had four years in the Navy, was a diver, and also liked to get naked. Mark also espoused the philosophy of the late James Dean: I am neither gay nor straight. If I were, I would always be missing half the fun.

On August 31, we flew out of Houston, over the Gulf of Mexico, over the virtually uninhabited jungles of the Yucatan Peninsula, and landed on the single airstrip of Belize City's international airport. Going through Immigration and Customs was easier than I expected. Walking out of the small fan-conditioned terminal and into the steamy tropical heat awakened me quickly to the fact that this was not Dallas, Texas. Sweat was trickling down my body in no time at all.

But there we were, our soon-to-be naked group, including Robert Steele, publisher of Naked Magazine, and his usual bevy of beauties, all sweating together. Soon, our ground transportation arrived, and in less than two hours we were on the ferry. As we rounded a point of land, the four-masted schooner, S/V

Fantome, came into view. To our comfort, the tropical heat stayed in Belize City.

For the rest of the day and evening we met most of the men on board. We were an eclectic group to say the least: young and not so young, beauties and not so beautiful, buffed and...well, you get the picture. As the week progressed, however, each of us found the beauty in all the others, whether it was on the outside or the inside or both. Any "attitude" became noticeable non-existent as we quickly realized that, for the next week, we were going to be daddies, brothers, sons and lovers, living together in relatively close quarters.

Also, the threat that the captain would lash us to the mast and flog us 'till our attitudes changed only appealed to a few. Of course, that never happened, so those few finally gave up their attitudes anyway.

The first night aboard erupted in the traditional game of "Musical Beds." As hearts melted and men found other men, luggage was re-packed and carried from assigned cabins to more amorous cabins, or at least more compatible ones. At the end of the night, the cabin roster was totally out of date. Somehow, everyone found their true love or friend for the week.

The cute little blond English Captain and the just as cute little female English Purser who were on the first cruise aboard the S/V Polynesia opted to rejoin our group on this cruise. They were very professional. They were also wonderfully fun, just like before. The only other woman on board was the Activities Officer. She also entered easily into the spirit of the cruise. Although they kept their clothes on, we loved them.

Obviously, if I have to mention the officers, I have to mention the crew. The crew was fantastic. They seemed to take care of every detail, from house-keeping, i.e. cleaning the cabins and the ship, to raising and trimming the sails, serving the food, and generally making sure that we were well cared for. Our nudity did not faze them. They made us feel at home and comfortable.

The Main Activities

The next morning, under power, we literally wiggled our way through the barrier reef east of Belize. It was intense, but exciting. Obviously the Captain and the First Officer knew what they were doing.

Although we seemed to sail back and forth, following the channel through the shallow reef, I never felt I was in any danger. When we finally cleared the reef, the sails were raised to the music of bagpipes and symphony and Amazing Grace, and we sailed across the open Caribbean Sea.

It was about that time when I discovered we were being escorted by a pod of porpoises. Watching their graceful bodies rise up out of the water was wonderful. Then I saw the small sailfish jumping out of the water, airborne for several seconds, then diving gracefully back into the water.

We sailed the rest of the day and night. The wind was brisk, but the ship was steady. As far as I know, no-one got sea sick. I slept peacefully with my sweetheart at my side. At daybreak, we sailed into the harbor of Roatan and anchored.

Roatan is the largest of a small chain of islands off the coast of Honduras. Since we had sailed from one country into the waters of another, Annie, the Purser had to go ashore and clear us. No problem.

We had a wonderful breakfast, and then divided into those who would dive, snorkel, and those who would tour the island. We chose to tour the island. It was beautiful, yet the poverty of the island was ever-present. The experience of touring an island with estates of the very rich and the clap-board huts of the very poor was unbelievable. The beauty of the island itself seemed to override all that. It was an unforgettable experience.

The town we landed in was called Coxen Hole. And it was certainly a "hole", if you know what I mean. It was a very old town with narrow streets and old buildings with tin roofs. But the locals were very welcoming and friendly.

And they know how to run a cafe. Before leaving the island, a few of us nestled into a waterfront cafe and ordered at least three different shrimp dishes. They were delicious but all were the same. A good lesson on how to have an extensive menu on a low budget.

Back on board, we got naked, lifted anchor and sailed in a brisk wind to Conchinos Grande, also known as Hog Island, in the Cochinos Islands just twenty or so miles off the coast of Honduras. Cochinos Grande is a small island inhabited by perhaps fifteen families who are almost never there, the owners of a small resort on the south side of the island and a small remote and primitive fishing village on the north side.

Our host, the owner of the resort, welcomed our nudity. Naked, we wander the beautiful beach, bought beer from our host, and had a wonderful time snorkeling the reef, just off shore of the island. The reef was pristine. The coral was beautiful and undamaged. The tropical fish were abundant. I could not imagine better, but "better" was still to come.

It was too bad that two of our number chose to ignore the strong advice of our Captain and wandered naked over to the fishing village on the other side of the island. This brought an encounter with the Honduran military. However, they arrived after we had time to get bathing suits on. The officer in charge was all smiles and certainly would have joined us under other circumstances. Nothing came of the incident. I waited to see if the two who broke the rules would be tied to the mast naked and flogged. Nothing happened. What a shame! I know one of them would have enjoyed it.

From Cochinos Grande we sailed in strong wind to Utila, the southern-most island in the chain that includes Roatan. It is a small-impoverished island with one main street along which are several dive shops and small unpainted, un-air-conditioned wooden hotels catering to divers. Diving is the main economy of the island and is spectacular. Although I don't dive, the maps in one shop showed 15 different dive spots and the proprietor said there were at least 15 even more spectacular dive spots that weren't shown. Four or so of our passengers did dive, and they reported that the diving was wonderful.

We saw the same type locals we had seen on Roatan: poor. But we also saw scads of bright-eyed and bushy-tailed young American and European youth, presumably from wealthy families, there for the sole purpose to dive. They lived in the same poverty as the rest of the islanders. But they looked healthy and had huge smiles on their faces. I presume their parents were happy to know they were on a small island somewhere off of Honduras. This may show my age, but I was amazed that they walked around in shorts with their underwear showing over the top, just like Dallas. Really cute!

That evening we again had strong winds. We left the harbor of Utila and set the sails for the long journey back into Belizean waters and Goff's Caye. This was perhaps the best sailing we had done.

I awoke about 2:00 in the morning and walked naked out onto the deck, then climbed the stairs to the main deck. The wind was up and the sails were full. The thrill of standing at the rail, feeling the full energy of the wind and listening to the sea below was simply awesome. The quarter moon and stars were brilliant. At that moment I felt what all sailors must feel--at one with the Universe, using the powers of nature to get from point A to point B. I felt I never wanted to get back to ... well, at that moment I forgot just where I had come from. The wind caressed my naked body and made love to me.

I turned and looked towards the bow and saw one lone black figure, hands on the wheel, guiding us safely across the Caribbean. I looked towards the stern, and saw three guys in the dim moon light, obviously helping the wind caress each other's naked bodies. I went back to my cabin to snuggle with Roger. I cannot tell you the kind of peace and love I felt at that moment, a moment when everything was absolutely right.

Goff's Caye is situated right in the middle of the barrier reef off the coast of Belize. When it first came into view, I could see no land, only palm trees sticking up on the horizon. As we sailed closer, still no land. Finally, I saw land. The island was no bigger than our city lot in Dallas. I can tell you it had exactly 18 palm trees, one palapa, and was approximately one foot above sea level at its highest point. Upon viewing the tiny caye from shipboard, I have to admit I was disappointed. But, as I said, the best was yet to come.

Upon coming ashore, the three of us donned our snorkeling equipment and entered the tepid sea. We quickly found it to be almost more than we could handle. Roger turned back. Mark and I tried to keep going, then turned back. It was not the sea. It was calm. It was not currents. They were basically non-existent. It was the fact that the coral and reef were mere inches below the surface and so profuse that we could not swim through them without damaging them.

After considering the situation, and because of my desire to take underwater pictures, Mark and I decided to try it again after lunch. Roger begged off. I had noticed there were "passages" of a sort among the coral.

Roger went back to the ship and Mark and I again entered the water with our facemasks, snorkels and fins. We saw beautiful red and black coral, brain coral and fans, totally undamaged by idiot tourists. Many times we reached a dead end, seemingly surrounded by coral, back-tracked, and found another way through the coral. There was no way divers could have gone into this area. It was a snorkeler's delight. It was by far the best snorkeling I have ever experienced.

The next morning, we sailed into the harbor of Belize City. After packing, we quickly found ourselves at the international airport, and just as quickly found ourselves airborne to Houston. And then home to Dallas. The cruise had already become a dream. But what a dream! Roger and I are already looking forward to Naked Magazine's next sailing adventure. I guarantee we won't miss it.

Life Aboard Ship

I have not even mentioned life aboard ship. It was also wonderful and interesting. First and foremost, the meals and drinks. All drinks were free, i.e. included in the price of the cruise. The food was not ho-hum, but it was not gourmet either. It was simple food cooked by a Caribbean chef, and much of it was quite good. But, then, what do you expect on an adventure!

The bar seemed to be always open. What better deal can you ask for! The drinks, whether or not alcoholic, were sumptuous and wonderful, and the bartenders were really cute and friendly. They were not going to be bed-partners, but we drooled over them anyway.

Ship's activities included a hilarious crab race, a body-painting contest, a costume "ball", and the Captain's dinner. It would have included more except for the rough seas, which were really more exciting than the rest of the stuff. The rough seas canceled the game of painting the name of a famous person on your ass, then you having to guess who you are supposed to be. With a few additional utensils, that could have really been fun. The body-painting took on both serious artists and persons who simply wanted to paint the body parts of whomever.

The results, however, were striking, and the awards went to the right guys. The body painting was both artistic and messy. And loads of fun.

The next night, off the shores of Utila, we had "Anything Goes" night. It was a costume party that simply wouldn't quit. It was wonderful, colorful, and exposing to say the least. Dancing went on and on into the night. The winners of the costume party certainly deserved what they got. Which was not much. But, as the saying goes, "a good time was had by all!" The Captain showed up in an Ester Williams swim suit with a British flag emblazoned across the front. I said he was cute and, boy, was he ever cute! His little tits just about did it for me, except that Roger was there. And my son Mark. How on earth would I ever be able to ... well, you know what I mean.

The last night aboard was the Captain's Dinner. It was a lesson in the preparation of a true Caesar Salad (only you who attended know what I mean) and adios, a happy and tearful time.

The rest of the time aboard ship was spent with old friends, new friends and the wonderful hosts. It was like going to camp all over again. Except much better. The guys on board were truly wonderful. The friendships made will probably be long lasting. No one that I know of left the ship feeling let down. The cruise was everything it was billed to be.

    The conclusion to all of this is simple. Would we do it again? Yes! Although I'm not a nudist or naturist (Roger is), I relish nudity in nature. Sailing on the open sea is by far the best example of getting close to nature. Being nude in the wind on a sailing vessel surpasses all other experiences. If you haven't done it, do it! You will amaze yourself! For those of you who have not experienced this kind of adventure, your missing a whole lot.

Larry P., Dallas, Texas

A Place in the Sun

Just after the war between Egypt and Israel (1967), I had an invitation to go on a Safari in Kenya. Cairo was an attractive respite in the long flight from San Francisco to Nairobi. I decided exploration of this ancient land was in order. It was a hot July and due to the diplomatic situation, there were only eight tourists in town, for whom there were 80 guides.

I selected a young man, about 20 who spoke remarkable English without any detectable accent. Since it is delightful to be able to understand one's guide, I had selected him for his linguistic skills, not imagining what other attributes were to be revealed.

We went down to the dock where his Felucca was tied and off we went for an eight-day sail on the Nile, for the absurd price of two packs of cigarettes (I would not engage in such a barter now). We sailed out in the breeze and on the water, which was a delightful relief from the heat. Nonetheless, I was quite over dressed and inquired of my sailor/guide if he would object to my shedding my clothes down to my thong. An engaging grin broke across his bronze face, revealing a perfect set of white teeth, as he welcomed me to get comfortable. He didn't know what a thong was, but was anxious to see and heartily approved. Upon noting my lack of tan line, inquired if I lived naked in California. Delighted by his bold inquiry, I affirmed his guess, realizing this was quite foreign to Egyptian culture. While taking off his shirt, revealing a surprisingly well-developed chest and arms, he suggested I shed the thong since he wanted me to be completely comfortable in Egypt. There was a wide bench which circled the boat, set low enough, providing privacy from the view of others sailing by. Not wishing to decline the opportunity for my first naked sun bathing in Egypt, I laid down and accepted his invitation to remove the thong. My guide, still smiling, stated that this was an extraordinary and rare event for him and he was enjoying my presence. I assured him the feeling was quite mutual.

As I lay on the plank looking up at him, he ran his fingers up my hairy chest and I noticed an increasing bulge in his khaki shorts. I explored up his muscular bronze calf and beneath his shorts and discovered an absence of underwear. By this time his grin was wider than ever, so with my other hand I reached for the drawstring that would release his shorts. He nodded agreeably and down they slid, revealing the most massive, erect phallus for such a short lad. His fingers migrated down to my pubic hair as mine moved upward towards his.

At this point we came to a jolting halt, almost throwing both of us onto the floor planks. Neither of us had been paying any attention to navigation and we had run aground on one of the many shifting sandbars in the Nile. I instinctively jumped overboard to push us off the sandbar as he pulled the centerboard up into the hull. In a minute the Felucca came around and was in motion once again. As I clamored back aboard, my new friend gave me a playful assist by grabbing my cock and giving it a good solid pull. That brought on mutual laughter, a great hug and continuation of our naked sail up the Nile. However, I denied myself the full expression of my desire for this most congenial Egyptian companion.

Loyal Reader

Dames at Sea

Joe had a sprinkle of freckles across his nose, big laughing brown eyes and curly blond hair. He was in his early twenties. I had met him in a campground where I worked, and I invited him home for the night. Home was my sailboat. He had never given any signs of sexual interest, and of course the matter had never crossed my mind. Honest.

Next morning I awoke to a vibration in the boat. It was strong enough to rattle the rigging. As I became more awake, I realized it was Joe, in his bunk, jacking off! As soon as I raised my head and looked at him, he stopped. Darn!

Later that day, we were sailing, out on the ocean, naked, of course, enjoying the peace and freedom that comes with naked sailing on a warm day, until I said, You woke me up this morning, jacking off. You were shaking the rigging.

I m sorry, Joe replied.

That s okay. I liked it. Why don t you finish? I offered.

He said, Okay, and stood up like a golden nude statue, his cock already getting hard. He walked past me, into the cabin, but turned to give me a profile of his naked body and full erection. A command performance and I hadn't planned any of it.

I couldn't join him, because I had to steer the stupid boat. Maybe that was okay because Joe was playing the part of the gorgeous, sexy exhibitionist to the hilt. His body was lean and graceful and he knew how to display it for maximum effect. He stood bent over, with his crotch thrust forward and upward. He stroked it slowly, enjoying every caress of his thick and full erection. As he neared climax, his eyes half closed and his whole body convulsed in the joy of ejaculation. He caught his cum in his hand, and when he was all finished he climbed out of the cabin and walked past me to wash it off in the sea water.

As we sailed back to the harbor, Joe told me that he had often gone on sailing trips and especially liked standing naked on the bow as the boat pulled into an anchorage, giving everyone in the anchorage a view of himself. I often fantasized pulling into an anchorage with Joe as my ornament.

B. G., Marina Del Rey, California

High School Memories

My first real experimentation with nudism occurred during my last year in high school. I was a very young looking, brown-haired, brown-eyed, 18 year old who was really getting in touch with his body. I barely had any hair on my chest then, but my legs were covered with a shag of fluffy hair. I'd always find myself stroking my leg hair whenever I wore shorts (I still do this today), and I guess I just became more and more comfortable with my body. I also became more willing to show it off.

Once I became bold enough to venture outside of the locker room, there was no telling where I'd turn up naked. I was involved in activities that kept me after school, sometimes until 9 o'clock at night. At that time, there were still handfuls of other students running around, as well as adults who came in for night classes, conferences, or other things.

I remember sneaking into the wrestling room, just so I could strip naked and lie on the mats, where only hours earlier, sweaty muscular boys had been grappling with each other. I'd get hard thinking about it, and just rub myself against the mats.

I'd also go into the weight room and use the various pieces of equipment or lie in the middle of the soccer field, masturbating as I looked up at the stars. No one caught me during those activities, but that wasn't always the case. In one instance, I was so overcome by the excitement of being naked in public that I completely lost track of my clothes.

It began as I was trying to think of a new place to get naked on school grounds. The sun had already set, so I thought

I'd try somewhere outdoors. I decided on the tennis courts, even though they were brightly lit. This being the suburbs, all parts of the school were relatively accessible. I went out on the back-court and stripped off my shirt and jeans. Standing in only my underwear, I put my socks and shoes back on, and listened carefully for noises. After a moment, I dropped my BVD's and stood proud, in the middle of the court, under a bright light. After walking around a bit, I noticed my growing, un-cut hard on. The urge came over me to take this experience a step further, so I found a gate in the fence that attached the tennis courts to the football field.

The gate was under the bleachers, so I quietly walked underneath them for a few minutes, again making sure that the coast was clear. Eventually, I walked up to the top of the bleachers, laid down, and began stroking my now very hard dick. It was a warm May night, which in Chicago isn't too warm, and I became covered in goose bumps as the occasional cool breeze blew over my sweaty body. I came, trying to keep as quiet as possible. I've always been a moaner. After a couple of moments, I realized I had nothing to wipe myself off with, so I just used my hands and tongue. It was the first time I'd ever had so much of my own cum. After this was all done, I was still feeling frisky.

I descended the bleachers and began running around the track that surrounded football field. Every ten feet or so, I would then enter a spotlight created by one of the bright lights mounted on the bleachers that shine down on the football field for night security. As I rounded toward the opposite side of the track, I was about to get my first taste of getting caught. The track and fields were located right next to a street that joined a small subdivision of homes to the main road. Sure enough, not one, not two, but three cars drove by as I cheerfully ran my private little race.

Although there were bleachers between me and the road,

they did little to obstruct the view. This was proven as the third car honked wildly as someone shouted encouragement out the window. I felt embarrassed and excited at the same time. Here I was, an 18-year old boy running naked on school grounds at 8:30 in the evening with nothing but shoes and socks. Luckily, the feeling of exhilaration won out or I'd have never tried anything like this ever again.

After I completed my lap, I sat on the bottom row of the bleachers to let the night air cool me. I was resting in a poorly lit corner, when I suddenly heard the gate creek open. I turned to see one of the school's nighttime security guards standing under one of the spotlights. Quickly but quietly, I lay face down on the floor of the second row of bleachers, watching the guard through the cracks as he surveyed the area. After a couple of minutes he turned around and headed back inside. I decided it was time to go, so I went back to the top of the bleachers where I had masturbated, but could not find my clothes. In all the excitement, I'd forgotten that I stripped on the tennis courts. For a moment, I thought I'd have to figure out a way to get home naked, but I soon located my clothing and got dressed. It's too bad, in a way, because sometimes it takes situations like losing your clothes to get you to the next step, but I gave myself many more chances which I'll share at some later date.

L.P, Chicago, IL

Locker Room Huddle

Dear Editor:

Enclosed please find a submission for your Encounters and Adventures section in your magazine. Though an infrequent reader (a friend subscribes), I very much enjoy the magazine, the pictures, and especially this section of the magazine.

    I am a published author of erotic fiction - but be assured, the story I have sent you is 100% true - hey, even I couldn't make this stuff up! At the same time, it isn't pornographic, but very alluring and erotic - and a true bonding experience. There was no wild sex ever involved - just a group of young, naked (mostly straight, even) guys bonding with one another and becoming a team. I think you II see what I mean when you read this piece.

    I'm not sure how it all started.

    I know that in my freshman year of college, our football team went 0-11. God, we sucked! We couldn't do anything right at all. We were just a small school, Division III, and football wasn't very important to the student body at all. But it still stung, and lot of guys ended up quitting. I thought about it, but I decided to stick it out one more year.

    We had a lot of freshmen on the new team, and a new coach, and somehow, between them, they had a lot of hope for the rest of us. I was the starting kicker that year, since our old kicker was one of the quitters, and frankly, I was feeling a lot of pressure as we took the field for our first game of the season.

When half time came and we were only down by a touchdown, though, the mood in the locker room was pretty upbeat. All of the freshmen kept poking, slapping, and charging each other, laughing and saying how they were going to kick ass in the next two quarters. I sat on a bench with three other upperclassmen - Abe, an offensive linesman; Gino, a wide receiver; and Mike, our senior quarterback - and we all began to ask ourselves could we maybe somehow win this one?

We played tough in the second half, and the score was tied with three minutes to go. Mike started a long drive that finally got us within field goal range with seventeen seconds left. It would be about a forty-yarder kind of long for me, but as I walked out onto the field to make the kick, I saw the hope in everyone s eyes. This would be our first win in over a year, and damn it, I was not about to fuck it up.

I though for sure it was gonna be short. It was dead on center but I hadn't caught enough of the ball on my foot and just knew it was going to be short. But it wasn't. It cleared the goal posts by just about five feet, but it was good. I had done it.

We'd won.

All I remember after that was hearing this huge roar from the other players and being lifted off the ground and paraded around our little stadium. There were a few interviews, lots of hugs and congratulations, celebratory kisses and pats on my rear. But I was in a total daze. The next thing I really remember is sitting in the locker room, still in all of my gear, with Abe, Gino, and Mike sitting across from me. I think we were all in a daze. Around us, the younger players hollered and whooped, streaking out of their pads and dashing off to the showers. But the four of us just sat there, dulled with victory, stupid grins splitting our faces. Shit Trevor, Mike finally said, you did it. No, man, I corrected him; we all did it.

By the time we got back to our senses the locker room was pretty much empty. The four of us finally stripped off our gear, our pads and uniforms, ditched our cups and jocks, and naked, we strolled towards the showers. We all got along one wall, turned on the streaming water, and just let it run over us.

There is nothing like a hot shower after a tough win on the field. I just sat there, the water streaming over my body, reliving that last kick over and over again, when I felt a strong hand clamp on to my shoulder. It was Mike. We just stared at each other, and finally, we embraced, like only two athletes sharing an amazing moment do. Gino and Abe joined in right away, and the four of us finally stood linked in a tight circle, one hand of mine around Mike's waist, the other straining to reach up around Abe's shoulders.

We just stood there, as different as four guys could be: me, a tall, lean blonde with a smooth, toned body; Abe, a huge guy, broad and hairy chested, and powerful as an ox; Gino, with his classic Italian looks, florid curly hair and sharp features; and Mike, our leader, a short compact muscular guy.

For the next half-hour we didn't move much at all, except for maybe to squeeze someone's shoulder, run a hand over their back, or pat their ass playfully. For the most part, though, the four of us just stood there, our heads bowed together, as if in prayer, holding on to each other in the warmth of the showers, the water still pounding allover our naked bodies.

God, just being there with them, it was an amazing experience. With our clothes all off, it was like we'd shed away all of the past, and we were just now there together, enjoying the icy tingling of victory and the steam of the shower.

That half-hour we spent under the shower like that just

brought us together, both as a team and as individuals. We made a pact; after every victory, we'd do just this. We'd come to the locker room, get naked, and get under the showers, holding on to each other and just being a team together.

I think what most amazed me about it was that it wasn't a sexual thing at all. Hey, I'd be lying if I said I didn't get turned on, didn't check out all those dicks, but those other guys, they were totally straight. It wasn't about sex; it was just about being together, and with our clothes off, it seemed to be even easier to get close to one another.

The next week we won again, an easier victory this time. Now we were 2-0, and the four of us waited impatiently for the locker room to clear so we could begin our post-game ritual. When the last freshman finally left, we quickly stripped out of our clothes, turned on all the showers, and stood together underneath them. We were there an hour this time, until our skin began to prune up; never talking, never saying a word, just holding on to each other's bare form and learning about being a team.

The next week we lost an away game; no ritual, but the week after that we won, also away. We rode the bus home, impatient. We'd already showered at the other team's site, of course, but we still had our ritual to complete. When we got back to our college we went straight to the stadium, went straight to the empty locket room. We stripped off our street clothes. Abe turned on all the showers, and we piled in again.

The noise from the showers was pretty loud, and if anyone ever walked in, we definitely wouldn't hear them until it was too late. We had never considered this, though, so when our assistant Coach Shepherd walked in that afternoon, we didn't notice him at all until we heard Hey! What are you guys doing in there?

Instantly we broke apart and faced Coach Shepherd. Standing alone, without my teammates, I really felt vulnerable and, well, naked. Coach stood there in paints and a polo shirt, staring at our naked forms and barking at us. Damn! I heard the showers from the hall and wondered what was going on in here, but I didn't think I'd see this! It's not what you think, Coach, Mike said. The four of us stared at each other should we tell him?

I'm waiting, Coach said. Finally I bit the bullet. Coach, its like this after every win, we wait until everyone leaves, then we come down here and do this. It s not sex or anything - it s just our way of being together after we win. Naked? Gino shrugged. Then it's like there's nothing between us, Coach, he said. Come on, Coach, Abe jumped in, I mean, like, after last year and all - we never thought we d be 3-1. We're winning!

And this - well, this is just how we celebrate. Is that so weird? Coach eyed us all for a minute. Finally, he smiled. I guess it's not that bad, he said. Athletes always do weird things anyway, right? He laughed. Carry on, men, he said, turning to go. Hey Coach? I said. He turned to look at us again. Join us?

Coach paused. Why not, he said. Anything for solidarity. He shucked his clothes and moved between Mike and me. I wrapped my arm around his black skin; he smiled, showing me his pearly whites, and I smiled back. We all put our heads together and resumed our ritual.

When we'd finally finished, Coach spoke up. Guys, he said as he put his clothes back on. I think I see why you do this. Gonna join us next week? Gino asked. Coach grinned. Are you guys guaranteeing victory? he asked. You bet! We all responded together. We did win the next week, pretty handily, over a team that we had never beaten before. Man, were we on a roll!

The five of us waited in the locker room afterwards for our ritual, but one pesky freshman, a little towheaded blond named Josh, was waiting around. Finally, he came up to me. Trevor, man, he said, I want to join you guys. I don't know what you're talking about, I said lamely. Yeah, you do, he said, looking right at me. Where did you hear about it? I asked. Josh grinned. Around, he said. It s not a sex thing, I added. Josh nodded. I know, I know. I just want to be part of the team, that's all. I shrugged. Then you're in, I said.

Our numbers continued to grow like that. By the end of the season, in which we went 9-2, there were seventeen guys crammed into the showers after the games. Seventeen naked men, seventeen linked bodies, seventeen dangling cocks, and seventeen bonding guys. Not all of us were football players - there were coaches, three of the male cheerleaders, even a couple of alumni.

After our last game, one last victory, we spent almost two hours together in the shower. All seventeen of us, linked and naked. After a long period of silence, someone started singing our college fight song, and soon we were all singing, and laughing, and chanting together. We decided to keep the party going, so we headed over to one of the alum's houses, tapped a couple of kegs, and sure enough, eventually, we all shucked our clothes again. It was definitely different, sitting around this guy's living room naked rather than our locker room shower.

For one thing, it was a lot colder (it was, by this time, early December, and we were no longer in those nice hot showers;) for another thing, well, the season was over, and for a while, at least, the team disbanded.

After that night we never got together again. Mike graduated; Gino didn't play his senior year. The next year we had a more average season, going 5-6, and my senior year, we were

3-8. We never quite recaptured the intensity, the solidarity, the togetherness, if you will, of that one magical season. The ritual was never resurrected, and though I now had a year's supply of dates, I've never been able to capture a moment like that again, where a huge group of hot, naked guys came together, not over sex, but over teamwork, learning to be together, and simply getting to know each other. But surely, it is a time I shall never forget.

Thank you for this opportunity to write about a very interesting set of experiences in my life that had a very great impact on me and whole lot of other people.

Trevor C., Kingston RI

Run For Your Life

I'm a runner off and on. It used to be an act of great self-discipline. Go out and pound the ground, get hot, sweat, come in, take a shower, keep sweating, feel thoroughly trashed and tired out. It had better be good for my health - this masochism. Whenever I stopped, it could be months before guilt, for ignoring my body would force me back into the sweaty rut. A couple of years ago, in desperation after trying to overcome the usual inertia, I called up all the self-discipline I could muster and set my alarm for 5 a.m. Keep in mind, I am a night person and getting up early was unthinkable.

Could anything overcome the laws of nature and biorhythms? It was hard enough just setting the clock radio for that hour, what were the odds of moving when it came on? It did and I was cast lead - immovable - no surprise. Then, inexplicably, I jumped up, pulled on shorts and sneakers and headed out the front door. I was electrified, alive from a palpable energy in the air. I live in a beach town in southern California. This is one of those towns with small buildings on small lots packed side by side. There's always traffic and no place to park. Motorcycles rage away from the stoplights rattling the whole neighborhood and lots of barking dogs. Now though, it was peaceful, quiet, no one around, lights out in the houses. A special world I had never experienced. I ran to the beach, down to the edge of the water and along the gentle surf, among the scurrying shore birds, stars twinkling, moon light dancing with me along the water as I ran. I was hooked.

I like being naked. I have been to nudist parks, driven naked, been naked at the beach and have had a fun going naked lots of other times in a variety of places. So, the thought crossed my mind, I could run naked here. At least along the water. Running the half-mile to the beach through alleys, across a very wide, normally busy street, along and across other streets would be out of the question. But, along the beach, in darkness with no one else in sight. Why not? I'd have to run the route a couple of times first to make sure it would be okay.

Over the next few weeks I experimented with the time. I went out running and made note of how many people I encountered along the beach. Unfortunately, it was not uncommon to run into a romantic couple watching a full moon playing on the water, pre-dawn surfers, fishermen or someone with a loose dog or two, tearing into the surf. If nothing else, the lifeguards and beach cleanup crews could suddenly be upon me with headlights glaring.

I usually run about a 1/2 mile to the beach and at least a mile along the beach - so a good 3 miles round trip. I don't try to set speed records so I'm out there a good 40 minutes. The anticipation of running naked was building. I was now taking my shoes off at the edge of the sand and leaving them next to a condo. Before long I was pulling my shorts off and running with them in my hand so that I could cover up or pull them on, depending. The thrill of running naked - seeing how far I could go - had me setting the clock radio and springing out of bed. Altered biorhythms - regular running how about that?

In the coolness of the morning air, although I perspired, I always seemed to be refreshed - not exhausted and enervated as before. This inner desire to be naked began to wrestle down my anxiety about getting caught. I would leave my house, hold my shorts in front of me and run all the way to the beach or until I needed to pull them on - which often happened. There are a lot of very bright streetlights and safety lights along the way. I am not into this to be an exhibitionist. I don't want to run into trouble. I am married and when I told my wife about how exhilarating it was to run naked she became upset - worried that someone might beat me up or the police might arrest me. I am very happily married and didn't want to threaten that relationship nor fall victim to her fears but it did make me nervous.

When I was carrying my shorts, I had a safety net. Most of the time I was just holding them up in front of me, sometimes twisting them around to cover my ass if passing someone. I'm talking exceptionally dense housing, lots of streets and intersections and traffic 24 hours a day. My heart began to pound over the thought of leaving my shorts somewhere and running with no safety net at all. I began to think of doing this part way down the beach. I'd drop my shorts and run the rest of the way, barefoot and totally naked with nothing in hand to protect me if I met people or the headlights started bearing down on me. The feeling of freedom, of being into my own was overwhelming. I had just reached the point where I would run to the beach without covering myself up and leaving my shorts with my shoes at the condos when I went to the newsstand one evening and stumbled upon Naked Magazine. I could not believe that other guys were doing the same thing.

I was totally psyched. It was after dark. I bought the magazine, jumped in my car, whipped my clothes off and drove home naked. I read about guys doing things without anything to cover up if caught. It stoked me.

That night I may not have slept at all - it didn't seem like it. There was a raging battle between two voices in my mind. The rational voice saying, No way.

Don't even think of leaving your shorts at home. The other voice saying, Do it! Other guys would. My heart pounded, my chest was tense, I kept trying to relax and get some sleep. I knew that if I didn't sleep I wouldn't be able to get up - period.

The radio came on. Yes, I was tired but I rose straight out of bed. I fumbled around and picked up my shoes, sox and shorts. I stole into the other room and put on sox and shoes. I picked up my shorts and headed for the front door. My gut was churning. The streetlights were brighter than ever outside. I was in control. I had my shorts in my hand, I would be okay. But, as I opened the front door, without thinking or having any control over it, my left hand threw the shorts on a chair. I went out, shut the door, looked around and started running. The feeling of freedom was far greater than I could have imagined. I trotted up my street and into the brightly lit alley, across the first intersection and half way down the next block when, bam, around the corner at the other end, a giant pickup with super bright lights aims right for me. In this maze of streets and alleys, there is a side alley that I duck into, back into the corner of a garage with bright floodlights on me but out of sight of the truck - unless he drives his truck down this alley for a look. The truck brakes, the driver guns the engine again and again and finally roars off. One down, how many more?

Some other force is in charge. I do not turn back. I run off. Three more short blocks and almost at an intersection when another pickup swings into the alley - spotlighting me. No choice. I jam my hands down in front of me and keep running. No problem. Now, I'm at the 7 lane wide street that is my biggest worry. I wait behind shrubs till it seems clear. I make it! Up the street, up the sidewalk of a walk street, across another busy street, past houses and condos to the sand yeah! I take off my shoes and sox, run way down the beach, further than usual, and then realize that it's now later than usual - people will be out on the streets and the sky will be getting light.

Oh, oh. I turn back, get to my shoes and put them on. I pass condos, down the Walk Street, cross the first street, continue but pull up short near where I have to turn onto the next street. Whoa! I see a guy in a parked delivery truck, window rolled down. I'm in luck. I spot him in time and there is a tall shrub that I duck behind. But I hear, What are you doing? I can see you. What? I stoop and see that the shrub is narrow at the bottom and fans out near the top. I am hiding only my head - the rest of my body well lit by bright streetlights. I line up better behind what little shrub there is and hope this isn't the guy who is going to teach me a lesson.

After a couple of verrrrrry long minutes, he starts up and slowly eases down the street. Now what? I have to go down that street, cross the wide street and make it down the alley across many more intersections. Would he circle around? Yet, despite the questions and the anxiety in my rational mind, I am filled with confidence and not caring.

I watch for traffic, dodge here and there and fly all the way back to within a block of my house when a small car pulls in at me. Who cares? I am invincible. I drop my hands and race by, turn the corner for home and stride through the door. Euphoric? Ecstatic? On a high? Words only hint at how I felt.

Later, I toughened my feet so I could run totally naked - even barefoot, all the way on pavement as well as on the beach. But, that and many other incidents would turn this letter into a book. I look forward to each issue of Naked Magazine to get more ideas. And, a book might be fun!

Anonymous

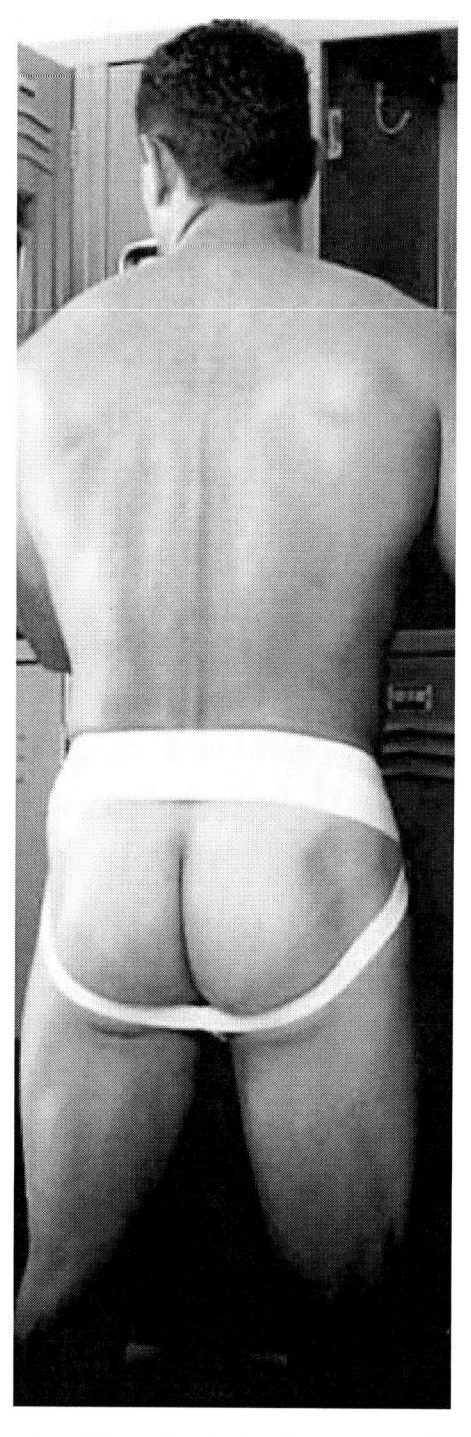

Serial Display

I've long enjoyed being exposed before appreciative audiences. Often, I plot my displays in advance and commit myself to their complete performance. I find that my hormones dictate bolder plans for nudity than I might otherwise accomplish. I was in Florida, staying at an exclusively gay motel. This was not a walled, clothing optional resort, but rather a 50's style motel, wrapped around a complex containing a coffee shop, gay bar and pool. The entire complex and pool were accessible to anyone on the street and parking lot. These facts didn't inhibit me as I made my plans for exposure.

In this case, I drafted a plan for serial display and committed myself to fulfill the plan to completion. I was to spend the afternoon by the pool and was to return to my room every thirty minutes. I would start wearing a skimpy bikini and with each trip would be required to change to an even more revealing swimsuit (I had several with me). Four levels of exposure were required. No towels or other clothing would be allowed. I checked into my room, on the second floor, some distance from the pool.

Standing in front of the open window in my room, I stripped naked and searched my luggage for the first swimsuit. It was a bikini with very narrow sides, skimpy butt coverage, and an unlined pouch that allowed my cock to flop lewdly from side to side with every step. I walked to the pool and began to enjoy the sun. I noticed that the bar had very large windows that overlooked the pool area (although the deep tint prevented those of us at the pool from knowing when we were being watched from within the bar).

After thirty minutes, I returned to my room and stripped naked while I examined my next swimsuit. It was an unlined thong. The waistband was only a half-inch wide and butt coverage was negligible. The tiny pouch barely contained my genitals and most of my pubes bristled over the top, exposed. I estimated that it covered perhaps half as much skin as the first suit. I returned to the pool area - now wearing the skimpiest suit of any man there - and enjoyed the warmth of the sun on my butt. I took a short swim and enjoyed knowing that the thin fabric was clinging to my cock as I climbed out of the pool.

As I neared the end of my thirty-minute exposure, I became quite anxious about what was to follow. I had committed myself to wearing a very small g-string - a thin white piece of nylon, just over 4 squares, shaped into a pouch and attached to a thin elastic waistband. If I were completely soft, I knew that the pouch would barely cover my cock and balls, but would inevitably leave my pubes exposed. An engorged cock, however, could not possibly help but be revealed. As I considered this, I felt my cock begin to swell and visibly tent my thong. Partially hard, I examined the small piece of fabric that I had promised myself that I'd soon wear.

Predictably, the pouch of the g-string was clearly too small to provide coverage of my turgid cock; a full inch of cock root was exposed. And I appreciated the total nakedness of my ass. I found the thought of being exposed in public like this intensely erotic and felt my cock stiffen more, stretching the skimpy pouch. But I had promised myself that I'd fulfill this dare. So exposed, I strolled back to the pool. My initial apprehension dissolved as I became comfortable with the exposure naked but for an elastic strap, and a small pouch that only partially covered my genitals. I swam in the pool for several minutes, feeling the drag of the water push the pouch down further, threatening complete removal. I promised myself that I'd climb out of the pool without adjusting the g-string, no matter how much slippage had occurred. I strolled back to my chaise, aware that the wet nylon was clinging to my cock and balls and was pleased with the substantial slippage of my G-string. I lingered by the pool for nearly an hour during which I was somewhat rewarded, when a waiter delivered a beer from an anonymous admirer from the bar. It wasn't complete yet. I had committed myself to yet another level of exposure. I again returned to my room. I had nothing to wear that was skimpier than the g-string. I had committed myself to total nudity.

Having just partially exposed myself in my g-string, I might have thought that being nude wouldn't be much more of a challenge. Yet standing naked in front of my window, I contemplated my plan, recognizing the difference the absence of the g-string would represent. Basically, I was going to walk naked through the public parking lot of a gay motel, expose myself completely before strangers and unknown others, watching from the bar, without even so much as a towel to provide coverage.

Obviously, my cock and balls would be on complete display. Without a g-string, I'd experience the sensations of my cock swinging from side to side with every step. There would be no escape from the display, even if I were to choose to end it. And I knew from experience that being exposed totally nude significantly increased the risk of developing a public hard-on. Part of me was trembling at the thought of what I was about to do, but I also felt my cock swell and stiffen. I opened the door to my room and stepped out onto the walkway, stark naked.

I was amazed at the eroticism of being nude in this situation. I enjoyed the feeling of the sun on my body and my turgid cock swinging freely as I walked down the stairs, across the parking lot and to the pool. I returned to my chaise in full view of the windows of the bar, wondering who was inside watching me and trying to imagine their reaction. I sprawled out, legs spread, cock and balls fully exposed to the warm Florida sun warming my bare genitals. I swam in the pool and found excuses to wander about the deck, enjoying the contrast between my nudity and the coverage of other guests.

I stayed naked by the pool well beyond my required thirty minutes, enjoying the conversation and wandering eyes of other guys who approached me to chat. I stayed by the pool throughout the entire afternoon before returning to my room. I really needed to get off, but decided to save it and increase my excitement and put my thoughts toward how I would expose myself that night, but that s another story.

Paul M., Oakland, CA

Stripped Naked

I wanted to write and tell you how much I enjoyed the Encounters and Adventures feature Mud Fight in your Vol. 4, Number 3 issue. Great stuff and right up my alley of interest. I am a very avid nudist, exhibitionist, body builder, sun worshipper, and wrestler. I'm in my mid-twenties, good looking, and have competed in numerous physique contests. Smooth and tanned, I enjoy showing off my body on the beach, by a pool, in the gym, the competition posing stage and just about anywhere I can. Although I enjoy full nudity, I am also turned on by wearing bikinis, thongs and G-strings. In fact, I often prefer going around in a revealing and teasing G-string rather than fully nude. I love wrestling while nude or while wearing skimpy attire. The Mud Fight article reminded me of so many such encounters I have had, particularly while enjoying a day on a stretch of beach.

Some of these wrestling encounters were with friends I was with that particular day but, more often, they were with total strangers who came upon me on location. Seeing my body-builder's naked or near naked body, seems to bring out the competition instinct in others. Some of these wrestling encounters were in good-natured, athletic, competitive fun; others were less than friendly and got rather nasty. However, all of these wrestling experiences have been something I find exciting to remember and I look forward to future such nude competition. I am, at this time preparing myself to live out for real one of my most sensual fantasies.

Believe it or not, I want to experience the following. I am a young, handsome, muscle boy professional wrester competing before a huge crowd in a foreign country. I enjoy teasing the fans and taunting my opponents by wrestling in nothing but a G-string style bikini, a good tan, and some posing pouch. After some early victories and a reputation as a show-off and arrogant muscle boy, I meet my match one night and suffer a humiliating defeat. Before it is over, I end up stripped naked before the howling crowd of fans and find myself carried about the ring, thrown around and placed in one hold after another, all while totally naked. I know it sounds crazy that anyone would want to go through such humiliation but I find the prospect highly sensual in a scary sort of way. I am really going to hunt out this fantasy and am close to it now. I am an excellent wrester but have added to my abilities by enrolling in a professional wrestling school. I wanted to learn some of the showmanship antics as well as pro style holds and throws. I have a guarantee from a European Promoter that will book me on their pro circuits of Europe, the Middle-East and Africa. He says that the fans in the arenas love to see young, good-looking, bodybuilder type wrestlers.

Unlike here, pro wrestling is geared toward adult entertainment and the fans look for rough, no-holds barred and sexy action. The promoter is aware of my fantasy and says such an outcome is bound to happen sooner or later. He says that particularly in some African arenas, if a European (or American) wrestler competed as a bodybuilder wearing very skimpy attire, one of the local wrestlers will do anything to make the wrestler look foolish. The promoter says some of these arena matches enforce no rules and a wrestler would think nothing of stripping his opponent, particularly if their opponent is European in origin and is brazen enough to wrestle in a very brief outfit. I'm really excited about this and I'll let your magazine know the outcome.

J.R., North Carolina

What Will the Neighbors Think?

I just had to take a moment and let you know how much spice you have added to my life. I had always suspected that I was a nudist at heart, but your magazine has taken me gently, step by step into a new and exciting way of life. I don t even remember how I first discovered your magazine, but I know I subscribed without hesitation. I have since discovered many new ways to approach life.

First, I learned of nude vacation destinations and persuaded my partner that we should broaden our horizons. We were both a bit apprehensive at first, but before long I was enjoying the sun warming my privates and my partner was enjoying watching all the beautiful men in their natural state. Although he did not remove his trunks, he did seem comfortable with me doing so.

It turned out to be a great vacation and ten months later we were back for more. After experiencing the wonderful feeling of being naked in the sun, I decided I did not want to wait for vacations once or twice a year in order to do so. So I began drafting out ideas that would enclose our back yard to create enough privacy to enjoy the great outdoors anytime I wanted at home.

This was not an easy task and held special challenges. We live in a neighborhood of two story houses all nestled in a valley and our backyard is the second to lowest point in the valley. We also share a driveway with our neighbor to the left whose property is slightly above ours.

Finally it all came to me and work began. With cedar fencing, lattice trellises and vines all strategically positioned I was finally able to lay in the nude in my own back yard. The only space I was unable to block was the view from the deck of our neighbors to the right. They are a fun straight couple whom we have become good friends with. I had approached them with what I was planning and they said they would not care and it would not bother them. I expressed concerns of how their teenage children would respond, so they simply asked the kids right in front of me and the kids said the same, that it would be no problem. It wasn't. One hot day I was out on my deck when one of their teenage sons came out onto their deck while speaking on the phone to his girlfriend for forty minutes and in plain view of me. Of course we did not speak but the next day in passing, he just waived and said, Hi, naked man. How s it going? So I really felt comfortable now. This was going to be a great summer. And it was.

My partner is so good to me that the other night, I came home from work and walked into the house to find him wearing nothing but an apron, making my dinner. We had talked about having a naked night, in where we just go around our normal evening, only naked. But I never thought he would actually do it. It was wonderful. After he was done cooking, even the apron came off. I cannot describe how freeing and exciting I found this to be. I love looking at my partner's body and he must have found it exciting too because we had the hottest sex we ever had since our last trip to Palm Springs.

He appears to be getting into this naked-ness too because that night he suggested we have naked night at least once a month. I could do it every day, but I don't want to push him too far, too fast. I have not yet contacted the Olympians, the closest naked club to where we live, but I have a hunch that will be our next step. So a big thank you to all the staff of naked magazine for gently reassuring me and for adding so much spice to my life.

Michael, Tanned in Tacoma, WA

Beach Encounter

One day last summer I just didn't want to leave the beach. It was late afternoon when the sky, water, and air all were perfect, yet it was starting to feel a bit lonely with the beach so deserted. I'd already dressed in my cut-offs and t-shirt and had packed everything except the towel that I was sitting on. I told myself "just 10 more minutes."

After a while I noticed that an attractive, athletic-looking photographer in white shorts was walking along the beach. He was so absorbed with the camera and the sea scene that he didn't see me at first. I called to say hello and I asked him about his photography. We talked for quite a while but when he noticed the time he said he had to get to the store before it closed. As he was leaving he asked if I wanted to go out to dinner with him that evening. He wrote down his name-- Todd--and the address of the beach house where he had a summer share--an easy walk. He suggested I come by for him around seven and said that we could walk to the restaurant from there.

I rang the bell at seven and was happy to be greeted by an athletic man at the door-but it wasn't my new friend from the beach. The guy explained he was Nick, one of Todd's housemates. My jeans started to feel tight in the crotch as I took in Nick's great body. Nick was buck-naked. He had thick gray hair, a marine-type haircut, a taut workout body, washboard abs, and a hose that hung from his loins in a magnificent arc. He welcomed me with a hearty "come on in." From the living room I saw another guy appear momentarily over at the entrance to the kitchen to give me a quick "hi." He was just as much a stud as Nick and just as naked. He was busy brushing a pair of black work boots. I learned that he was Nick's partner, Bart.

Nick told me to have a seat and said Todd would be home in a few minutes. He went into the kitchen to get me a cold drink. A few seconds later Todd came in--all dressed for dinner in long pants, a casual shirt, and a windbreaker. He seemed embarrassed. He said he was so sorry he was delayed and hoped it hadn't been too uncomfortable for me. He was a bit tongue-tied as he explained that his housemates never wore clothes around the place. I could see that Todd was eager to rush me off to dinner as Nick appeared with my soda.

I turned to Nick and said, "Sorry, I didn't know the rules of the house." I quickly stripped the clothes from my body until I was standing completely naked and erect in the middle of the room. As Todd's jaw dropped, Nick turned and asked him if he wasn't feeling a little out-of-place with the windbreaker and all. Nick then smiled and called to Bart to bring some margaritas out to the deck where we could all watch the sunset.

We sat in deck chairs and enjoyed the views--views of the sunset, the ocean, and of Todd undressing.

I confessed to the group that my evening strip wasn't just an isolated whim. I'd always been an avid nudist. Todd laughed with relief. It turned out he was a closet nudist and said he hadn't expected to run across other nudist guys so easily outside his household. We sat around swapping stories and drinking margaritas until one of the guys shouted "last one in the water has to get dressed."

The beach was about 150 feet away so we ran bare-ass down to the water in twilight-after all, none of us wanted to be the one to have to get dressed. We had an invigorating evening swim and came back to the house to settle in and swap more stories. After the hot summer day it was great to have the coolness of the evening settle on the skin and to be able to look at other naked guys enjoying the same thing. In fact, we were so relaxed we didn't want to venture out for food, so we just munched on chips and salsa into the night. It was the best beach day all year and it was the start of many return visits to the "naked beach house" where I'd learned to strip before even ringing the bell.

Unknown

Naked Yard Hopping

Everyone should be as lucky as I am to have a regular fuck buddy. Bobby and I get together a few times a month usually at his house when no one is home.

Last Saturday night we were having our usual spot of heavy breathing and as we were cleaning up we heard a car door close in his driveway, we quickly got our wits together, and he shoved me out the back door. This would have been fine but I was standing out in the backyard without a stitch of clothes. We were so concerned in getting me out of the house without being caught we just bolted and ran.

So here I was naked as a jaybird in the dark back yard and wondering what I should do next. I knew Bobby would come and rescue me but I didn't know what to do and where to wait for him so I just stayed put. I guess he was talking to his parents because it seemed like forever that I was sitting naked behind the bushes next to the back stoop. I was out there for about 45 minutes when all of a sudden another car came up the driveway. The headlights shined right up against the garage door and stopped right in front of it in the backyard about 10 feet from where I was sitting. It was his brother coming home from a date and all I could think of was to run out of the yard before I was caught bare assed naked in Bobby's back yard. So I quickly got up and ran through the bushes and ended up in the neighbors' back yard. I thought I was safe as I was slowly walking through their back yard when I tripped the motion detector light on the back of their house. The floodlight came on and my heart raced. All I could think of was running the hell out of there and getting some place dark and safe. I quickly ran to their back fence and jumped over it into the next yard.

Once over the fence I heard a dog start barking that was in that house and quickly a light snapped on and again I had to run to the next yard over another fence and finally nothing stirred and I was in a dark back yard finally safe behind some big bushes right behind Bobby's back yard. It seemed like forever that I was running naked through the world and had come full circle and now had to get back into Bobby's yard where I hoped he was looking for me with my clothes. I did go over one final fence into his yard and hid on the side of the yard behind some thick bushes waiting and looking for him to come out.

I have to say it was kind of erotic standing there with the soft bush brushing against my shaved balls. While I am not shy about being naked (in fact I'm kind of an exhibitionist) this wasn't the time or place! It was getting real cold out there waiting for him to come out and find me and I was experiencing major shrinkage when all of a sudden someone knocked me off my feet and right on my ass. I was in a state of terror as I was being knocked to the ground and held down when I heard this soft laughing from my attacker when I realized it was Bobby. I whispered "YOU ASSHOLE!"

He quickly assured me it was safe and he had my clothes. I was so relieved to see him and I got him naked too and we had another spot of heavy breathing right there in the bushes of his back yard. You could say we kind of fertilized the bushes!

John J.

The Ole' Swimmin' Hole

The fifty-yard walk from our farmhouse in Central Indiana to the barn convinced me that the day was going to be sweltering. I harnessed Beth and Star (our team of matched Belgian draft horses) and mounted Best, our Tennessee Walker, for the ride to the hayfield my dad and I were loading.

We usually used tractors but we liked to use our draft horses to keep them in shape for showing them at the county and state fairs.

With the tractor, Dad pulled the hay wagon under the hayrack harnessed to the horses, and we started around the perimeter of the field slowly, feeding the alfalfa up the rack to have it cascade over the top like a waterfall into the waiting wagon below. Within minutes, every piece of my clothing was soaked with sweat. We had the wagon loaded in about forty-five minutes so I unhitched the team from the hayrack, swung up on top of Tom's wide back, and started back toward the barn.

There was plenty of hay left to cut in another field, but it was too hot. Dad and I had decided that my brother, Thad, would unload the last wagon when he got home. We wiped, fed, and watered the team. After they cooled down. I wanted to go for a swim and invited Dad to come along. He declined my offer as he settled into a high backed oak rocker on our shaded front porch, moving slowly backward and forward. I mounted Best, tied a scrappy piece of towel to the saddle blanket straps, and rode toward the creek.

At Flat Iron Creek I looked down into the clean pool directly beneath the bridge. I could hear soft crackling as a trickle of water left the pool and slipped over the smooth stones. The pale green leaves on the poplar trees that lined the creek banks moved in the hot summer breeze.

I walked Best across the bridge and turned left down a gentle incline that was marked by tire tracks. The only sound was our feet softly passing over the cool grass. Upstream the bank got steeper and the tree branches reached across the narrow gorge to form a canopy over a shimmering, silent pool disturbed only by water bugs scampering over the mirrored surface. No bird songs sweetened the air. It was too hot.

During my nineteen years, I had often come here with friends to laugh and frolic. I even dreamed of leaving my virginity on the banks of this special place. I tied Best to a bush, ensuring that she was in the shade, and then sat in the grass and let my mind wander as I looked up at the leaves moving quietly thirty feet above. Minutes passed before a bee buzzing about startled me into consciousness.

My boots came off first, then my clammy white socks. I unsnapped the strap on my overalls and slid them off with my sweaty underpants, folding them over my boots. My striped cotton shirt was soaked with the sweat of hard work. I stood naked on the silent creek bank and then descended the makeshift stairs cut into the bank. The warm mud squished between my toes as I stepped into the stream. I dove toward a half submerged log. The water was perfect. I turned over and floated on my back.

I heard a laugh. With another stroke, I reached the log and propped myself against an exposed branch. The view downstream was obscured by trees whose roots no longer held them upright. They had fallen over but continued to grow, providing a curtain for bathers. I swam upstream, stepped onto a sandbar but the sand was too hot. Hopping around to get back to the water, I heard another shout and some laughter. I was sure I would know the people because I knew everyone in the vicinity who swam in the creek.

Without warning, a naked boy about eighteen years old swung out on a rope over my head and dropped into the water. Then another boy a couple of years older followed by a muscular man in his forties flew over me. The naked boys acted as if I was not there.

The hunky man yelled something incoherent as he released the rope and dropped into the water.

"Hello," I answered as he swam away.

It wasn't until a tanned hard body with short blond hair flew over me that the situation got intense. I was naked and excited. I quickly sank into deeper water, wondering who these people were and what they were doing in MY swimming hole. I turned to slip away downstream when the muscle man flew over me again. Seeing my imminent departure he yelled, "Nein, nein" and motioned me to join him. I followed him up the bank to a flat open space under a huge tree. The group, which included the four guys I had seen previously and one other equally endowed athlete, sat comfortably in the shade.

They remained nude and natural as if this were the way they always were. Everyone was blond-haired, blue-eyed, and very muscular. I must have had a puzzled look on my face because one of the boys mumbled and then I caught the word "Circus."

"Aw, yes," I said, relieved to know something about these people.

The older boy motioned for me to sit.

I immediately sat and arranged my hands over my excited manhood.

"Watch," the older boy said with a heavy foreign accent.

He and the others did a series of acrobatic tricks. There were several beautifully executed flips and tumbles. The climax was tossing the youngest boy to the top of a three-person pyramid. I imagined myself sitting on the mat watching the German Olympic gymnastic team doing floor exercises. I applauded. Suddenly as if signaled, the group dressed, talking loudly in their unintelligible language, and grabbed their bicycles.

I watched them walk their bikes up the incline by the bridge and turn south toward Fort Wayne. I dropped back into the grass and closed my eyes imagining wonderful things about the lives of those beautiful athletic guys.

Roars from a motor made me open my eyes. Thad drove up in our truck and yelled, "What the hell are you doing?" "I'm thinking about the acrobats."

"Sure," he sneered.

When Thad joined me in the grass, I told him about the intruders and the acrobatic performance they did for me. Then Thad stripped off his shirt and said, "Let's get in the water and cool off. It looks like you need it."

Seth N, Ft. Wayne, IN

Oil On His Hands

I was nude sunbathing poolside at Sea Isle, one of the fabulous clothing-optional guesthouses in Key West, reading Felice Picano's "Like People in History" and paying little attention to anything except the warm sun and the glorious blue sky.

The temperature was cooler than usual and, when the sun slipped behind a cloud, I reached for a towel to cover myself. I noticed that a totally tanned man with a well-defined torso and biceps was reclining two lounges from me. It was obvious that he must obsessively attend to his physical conditioning. I looked intensely at his smooth, freckled skin and thinning, blond hair. He turned his head and caught my gaze.

"How long are you here?" he inquired.

A friendly icebreaker question, I thought. "Four days; and this unfortunately is my third. I sure wish it would warm up since I have to leave tomorrow."

He moved in my direction and his smooth shaved manhood dangled before me as he straddled the lounge next to mine. I indicated that I had not seen him before. He told me he lived in Key West when he wasn't in the Alaskan oil fields. We discussed careers and occupations and became friends quickly. He had a warm natural way about him. I found out that Henry ("call me Hank") had spent fifteen years working for one of the world's largest oil companies with assignments all around the globe. He told me he had been downsized out of his job in the late 1980s and, since he was a committed nudist, he decided to move to Florida. As we talked, I found that he continued to consult for oil companies around the world and is gone from Key West six to eight months a year. Hank told me that he had a condo on nearby Truman Street.

He invited me for cocktails and hors d'oeuvres and suggested going out to dinner at Louis Back Yard where we could watch the stars on the water and the moon over Cuba. When the late afternoon clouds completely blocked by the sun, we parted.

After a long leisurely shower, I dressed in black silk slacks, a full cut white, open collared shirt and black leather sandals. I felt relaxed, sexy, and a bit of a voyeur as I walked through the quaint neighborhoods looking onto people's front porches and into their homes. Hank was naked when he opened the door. As I stepped from the cool evening air into his warm condo, I comfortably shed my clothes.

The decor of the condo mirrored his many work experiences. He explained that oil was pumped from the depths of Prudhoe Bay, Alaska, and that it was his job to see that it was transported safely hundreds of miles through the pristine Alaskan wilderness insuring that the fragile environment was not damaged. The trophies that adorned his walls included a massive baleen from a bowhead whale that was a curved cartilage cutlass fringed with thousands of fine black silk threads. The baleen's starkness was softened by the hide of a caribou that hung nearby. Another wall was decorated with ceremonial masks created by native Alaskans.

Hank told me stories of other trophies as we toured his home sipping chilled Dos Equis. We were having so much fun exchanging stories that it was time for our dinner reservation before we were ready. We considered calling and telling them we would be late but decided to call and cancel instead. Hank smiled and suggested that he would fix a simple salad. He set a beautiful table and the candles were flickering as he accented a bed of romaine with tomatoes, mushrooms, hearts of palm, and caribou sausage. He finished his "salade a l'Henri" with croutons, Greek olives, and fresh spicy vinaigrette. We ate and chatted like old-time friends. He asked if I would like a massage for "dessert."

I happily accepted and we traipsed upstairs to his massage table. The table was placed under giant photographs of stately derricks and great tankers carrying their black gold throughout the world. As I lay face down on the sheet-covered table, Hank told me that his massages required plenty of oil. It seemed appropriate that a man who had spent his professional life in the oil fields would use plenty of it.

Fortunately, he didn't use crude oil but rather rubbed his large, muscular hands with aromatic almond-scented oil and gently caressed me. From the first touch it was clear he was a skilled masseur. He gently worked his way from my shoulders down each arm to my hands. When he wasn't massaging me he was gently touching me. The occasional touch of his firm belly or his soft dick brushing my arm or my leg reminded me that he was naked, too. As he moved into position to rub my back I could feel the cool tip of his dick through the strands of hair on the top of my head. I kept thinking this was a fantasy (a perfect massage by a nude male masseur) but it was real.

With increasing frequency his hands slipped into my crack as he worked on my gluts. As his fingers caressed each leg, he gently grazed my sack. He sent shivers through my body as he softly brushed his fingertips over my slippery, receptive skin. His fingers were like the sable bristles of a fine brush applying the final touches on an oil painting.

I turned over and noticed his handsome face glowing with the sweaty dew of the physical intensity he was devoting to my pleasure. I relaxed as he kneaded my heaving chest. He told me he coveted the bushy hair covering my chest. He gently ran his fingers again and again over my oiled chest. His massage was never too hard but was always just firm enough to excite. His fingers moved below my waist. My legs were stretched and kneaded as if they were dough readied for the bread pans. I often opened my eyes to watch Hank's intense concentration. He massaged every part of me. We were two men from different parts of the country brought together for this one special night. He caressed my dick and when I came like the oil gushers he knew, we cuddled.

He was tender and sensitive and I was too. When someone is in sync with your thoughts and your pleasures, knows what's in your head and then touches your soul, what could be more perfect? Hank and I had touched, we'd caressed, and we'd made love.

We embraced. The scented oil mixed with all the exotic fragrances of the evening as I walked out into that paradise that is Key West in the moonlight.

Seth Wallace, Oak Brook, IL

Caught

I like to get naked and go where men can see me. I guess you could say I'm an exhibitionist. And at six feet tall with a 33-year old, 170-pound body that I work out regularly, I know I have a body that is meant to be appreciated. I have an uncut dick that's not only a "show-er" but also a "grow-er" with a pair of shaved low-hanging balls.

I live in the "gay village" in Montreal, Canada, so it's no problem finding an audience.

One very hot, humid July night with a full moon rising, I was drinking vodka on my front porch while watching the boys cruise by. After a while I got pretty tanked, but not drunk-just intensely sexual. That's the way hard liquor makes me sometimes, not swaying or blurry, just horny and daring.

"It's time for a walk," I told myself. So I left the house, wearing nothing but a pair of sneakers and an old worn Speedo. I bound my cock at the base with a leather thong so it lay swollen horizontally across the loose-fitting Speedo. Anybody standing in front of me could look down and see my big semi-erect dick lying there like a dog-I couldn't let it get real hard because then it would stick straight up and out!

I prowled around the neighborhood like that, acting as natural as anything, watching guys gawk at my Speedo and what was in it. So many men love to look at stuff like that but most are too chicken to do it themselves. I became even more lusty after strolling through the streets for a while with the hot humid night air clinging to my skin. A few guys already had a good look down my Speedo and made their excitement quite obvious, but I wasn't into merely getting groped in the alley-I wanted to spread my lust around.

When I got to a dark street near the bridge that goes over the St. Lawrence River, I wanted to get completely naked so bad that I couldn't wait anymore. I pulled my Speedo completely off- I even undid the thong around my cock and bundled them into my hand. I proudly strutted down the street with my semi-erect cock swaying back and forth. Man, I felt so free, so good, and so sexual! I walked to the end of the block-I don't think anybody saw me-and when I got to the end, it occurred to me that it would be a thrill to run across the bridge naked. So I slipped my Speedo back on to cross a busy street and headed up to where the sidewalk of the bridge started. Since this was a small park I felt it was okay to get naked again so I hid my Speedo under a tree. I started jogging along the bridge as though it were perfectly normal to go running naked (which it should be).

I hadn't gone fifty feet before I noticed red lights flashing. I was streaking across a bridge in front of cops! I quickly turned around and ran as fast as I could back to the little park, down a couple of streets, behind the fence of another park and past an outdoor party. I hoped they saw me, a naked blur rushing by! I stopped to catch my breath behind some hedges in the park.

I thought it would be fun to return home like that-only a few streets away-but I had the brilliant idea that I should try to retrieve my Speedo, as a challenge. So I strolled back to the "scene of the crime" only to find that three cop cars had converged on the site. Imagine six cops hunting down a naked man! Figuring they were all looking for me over at the one end, I tried to get my Speedo from where I had hidden it on the other side of the park. I streaked to some fir trees and crawled, army style, to the next cluster-I wasn't even sure where my Speedo was. Then all of a sudden it didn't matter anymore: a searchlight flooded my path-I was caught!

I stood up and surrendered to the authorities. And this is where the fun really began. I got to stand there, stark naked, as the cops surrounded me. They immediately handcuffed me. Mmmm. There I was, completely naked wearing only sneakers-and now, handcuffs! The younger one was about 22 and kind of dewy looking. He acted really straight-as though this was just another bust. The older one, about my age, was dark and sexy and was making jokes about it. I thought it must have been a change of pace for him to pick up a nudie; and he even said I was good looking. Maybe the naked people they usually picked up were ugly. The other cop asked me why I was doing this. I looked up at the full moon. Somehow they looked as if that was a reasonable explanation.

Next, they hustled me into a patrol car. They covered me up with a blanket and kept trying to find my clothes. They brought back jeans, sneakers, and all sorts of dirty clothes they found hidden in the bushes. I denied ownership of any of them, and I knew they'd never find my tiny Speedo in the dark.

Eventually they drove me to the station. On the way the sexy one made jokes. The whole while the blanket they gave me kept slipping farther and farther down my shoulder. Of course, I couldn't pull it back up, even if I had wanted to!

At the station, while I stood there with this dumb blanket slipping down my shoulder, the cop who said I was good looking said it again and made a cock sucking pantomime while jerking his head toward his partner, as though telling me I should suck off his partner. Then the sexy one whipped the blanket off me, as though I were supposed to feel humiliated. For me it had the opposite effect. There I was, completely nude again except for sneakers and these oh-so-sensual handcuffs on my wrists in the middle of a police station full of hot, sweaty cops. What a triumph! Can you think of a more desirable audience for showing off? What an opportunity for an exhibitionist!

I just stood there, looking around at all those hunks looking back at me, remembering what the cop said about my being good looking, getting so excited that it was beginning to show. My dick was standing at half-mast.

After they signed me in, the sexy cop and his partner hustled me down the corridor and out of the desk area, my dong swaying freely before me. My keeper made me take my shoes off and he removed the handcuffs. I went inside the cell. Now I was completely naked, in a police cell, in front of two hunky cops, with a swelling dick. The one who made the blowjob joke took a good look, and had a sort of frustrated look on his face. Who knows; maybe he was interested?

The cell was all ceramic tiles, including the bench. And since it was just as hot inside the jail as it was outside, the first thing I did was lie down on the floor in that hot, muggy jail cell, with nothing touching my body but those cool tiles, and beat off. I dozed off after that and it must have been a couple of hours later when my "friends" came back with ambulance drivers! It looked like I was going to be taken to the hospital and the only reason that I could think of was for a psychiatric check-up. The cops must have thought I was running around naked because I was nuts! Yeah, nuts about getting naked!

The ambulance drivers had me get on a stretcher and they covered me with a sheet and wheeled me into the ambulance. At the hospital they left me in a corridor for a few hours. Before dozing off, I looked around at all the really sick people and thought, "This is stupid! They have me waiting here for medical attention while these people really need it."

When the shrink finally came around and woke me up, I

was quite sober but rather groggy. All I wanted to do was go home. I convinced him that I tried to run across the bridge naked only because I was drunk and that, otherwise, I was quite normal.

The shrink agreed and let me go, but when I pointed out that I had no clothes, the staff didn't know what to do. I got excited when it looked like they were about to let me leave the hospital naked. Eventually they gave me some hospital gowns-you know, the kinds that are always open at the back and a taxi voucher. But I decided to walk home dressed in those hospital gowns.

Once I got home, I was wide awake and still horny and excited from my adventure with the cops. So I took another hit of vodka, put on a pair of shorts and went outside. In the park nearby, I dropped the shorts in some bushes and walked around the block like that, buck naked, just to do it again and defy the system that says you can't show your penis.

John W., Montreal, Canada

Gratis Solarium

I was in Germany on a business trip and I knew that I wanted to expose myself at Gratis Solarium. I delayed my departure for a day so I could travel by train to Hannover. Although I didn't arrive at the solarium until after 11:00 p.m., the lobby was still crowded with a mixed audience (mostly men in their 20s).

Standing in the waiting area, I recognized that I was different from the other clients. I was wearing my business suit. I appeared at least a decade older than most of the other customers who were much more tanned than I was. My poor language skills with German contrasted with their fluent conversation. However, from the little that I understood, I gathered that many of the customers were university students.

I knew that I wanted to be assigned to one of the rooms with a camera in the tanning bed. With what I remembered of my high school German, I tried to ask the woman at the reception counter for "cabin 2 or 6," but received only a smile in reply. The flow of customers in and out of the cabins was surprisingly brisk. After only about 15 minutes, I was directed to cabin 2. I gave the receptionist an appreciative smile, and felt my face blush, as if embarrassed that my "secret" interest in exhibitionism had been discovered.

Cabin 2 was quite small but neat. The horizontal cylindrical tanning machine occupied the right side of the cabin. The upper half of the tanning bed was open, displaying the rows of lights that would soon encircle me. The narrow space on the left side of the cabin was bare but for a small chair. There was a mirror on the wall and below it, a small shelf with body lotion and a spray for cleaning the tanning bed. I knew where the camera would be: on the ceiling directed at the only open space in the cabin. I felt anxious, but also felt a sexual charge. I was eager to strip naked, and show every inch of my body to an anonymous, worldwide audience.

I wanted to get naked immediately, and remain naked as long as possible. I took off my coat, then my shirt and tie. Only when I stripped to the waist did I bother to hang these items on the back of the chair. I undid my slacks and slipped them down to mid-thigh, before stopping to remove my shoes and socks. I removed my slacks then immediately dispensed with my briefs. Within 60 seconds, I had gone from fully dressed to completely naked. I was turned on by my nudity, and my penis reacted accordingly. I didn't mind-in fact, I had been hoping that I'd get hard. When I did get hard, I felt an even greater sexual charge about how I displayed myself.

Now that I was naked, I explored the small cabin, and pretended to find the tanning bed in need of cleaning. I realized that I would now be visible on the camera at the base of the tanning bed, as well as the camera on the ceiling. The former would display a close-up of my face, and I felt a momentary panic. "What if my family or boss is watching?" Reality was reassuring: if my boss watched Gratis Solarium, I would not need to be concerned about his reaction. I liked the fact that my stiff penis was being displayed on the camera in the tanning bed.

I climbed onto the tanning bed, and closed the machine. The lights were surprisingly bright, warming my nude body. I spread my legs, allowing my audience a view of my genitals from below. My cock flopped up against my belly rock hard. My nudity, the lights, the warmth, and the knowledge that I was being watched by unknown hundreds or thousands of men from around the world all contributed to my arousal.

The fifteen minutes passed too quickly. I was reluctant to dress; I wanted to prolong the display of my nudity. And I needed to get off. Standing in front of the mirror, I jerked myself. After only a few strokes, I came. Later I realized that my position in the room almost certainly put my ejaculation outside of camera range.

Still naked and dripping cum, I cleaned the lights of the tanning bed. Only then did I dress, prolonging my genital exposure by first putting on my shirt and socks. I returned to the lobby, pleased that I had experienced my first public ejaculation.

I have another trip to northern Europe later this year. I know that I'll return to Hannover. This time, I want my ejaculation to occur in the tanning bed. Watch for it.

Unknown

Gym Exposure

My favorite gym was one of the few gyms around the city that was still open exclusively to guys, and good-looking guys at that. In fact, on hot days the pedestrians would stop on the street to look up and see the muscular hunks leaning out of the second-story windows between sets.

For me, the locker room was always part of the incentive to get my ass over to the gym and work out. The locker room was a lively place where guys would start conversations just to watch each other strip down.

One Saturday, after a sweaty workout, I was headed to the showers but saw there were no towels left on the shower shelf. I did an about-face and rushed out to the front desk buck-naked. The front desk was at the far end of this large exercise room. It was also the place where the public entered the gym and where non-members would wait to meet their gym friends after the workout. Anyway, the workout floor and the desk area there certainly weren't intended to be clothing optional. When I reached the guy at the desk I simply said "no towels." Without missing a beat, he reached behind the counter and produced a clean towel for me.

With no attempt at covering my goods, I slung the towel over my shoulder and walked back across the workout floor with my pointer at half-mast. That's when I realized what a turn-on it is to be the lone naked guy in a room full of athletically dressed men.

Paul, New York City NM

Total Exposure

Dear Naked Magazine:

I have been an avid reader of your magazine for several years. My favorite part is the personal accounts in the Encounters and Adventures section. I look forward to reading these features each time I receive an issue, and am always amazed and intrigued by the stories from guys who get naked in public places. Mostly, though, I am inspired by these tales. It is the idea that these naked adventures are carried out by ordinary guys, just like me, that gave me the inspiration to orchestrate my own adventure.

For several months I had been formulating a plan to appear completely nude in public-an event worthy of a letter to your publication. Until recently I had never found the courage to follow through with full nudity in public, that is until an unusual Thursday evening last month.

I had just finished re-reading one of your reader's stories- the one from the guy in California who runs nude early in the morning. His story was so inspiring that, before I knew it, my body began yearning for the same feeling of exhilaration and my mind began formulating the way to achieve it. I stood naked in front of my mirror examining my smooth, slender body and wondered how it would feel to expose myself totally in public.

I live in Dallas where much of the year the air at night does not dip below room temperature, so I threw on minimal clothing that would be easy to get in and out of. At around 12:30 a.m. I started to walk toward my car not knowing where I was headed. I passed the common laundry room of my apartment complex and remembered I needed to wash a load of clothes. My first opportunity for public nudity had presented itself.

The laundry room is centrally located in my complex and for security purposes has large glass windows on two sides. It is very visible to a few apartments and a side street. At this time of night it is especially visible because of the overhead fluorescent lights. Standing in front of the washers I decided the clothes I was wearing needed washing. I kicked off my sandals and without so much as a second thought removed my T-shirt, shorts and underwear, threw them into an empty washer and started it. Completely nude I walked over to the coin-operated laundry dispenser, enjoying the feeling of the cold tile beneath my bare feet. I bought a pack of detergent and threw it into the washer. One of the dryers was spinning so at any moment another resident could have walked in on me.

At this point it hit me that I was standing in my own laundry room totally nude and with no dry clothes or a backup plan for how to get out of this situation. Here was another opportunity for public nudity; I could walk naked back to my apartment across a brightly lit parking lot and courtyard, with nothing to cover myself except my wallet.

The stairs leading to the back door of my apartment are about 15 paces away from the laundry room, diagonal across the parking lot and courtyard. With my sandals back on and wallet in hand I peered out across the complex. I stepped out onto the sidewalk and instantly felt the rush of having my dick, balls and ass completely exposed to the warm night air and to anyone who might be watching. Instead of running, as I thought I might do, I savored the walk and enjoyed the feeling of my newly freed cock swinging from side to side. I reached the top of my stairs without being seen. But uh-oh! In my haste to leave the laundry room I had left my keys on the washing machine.

Shielded from view, I stood nude in my stair vestibule and wondered (and secretly hoped) if a second trek across the courtyard and parking lot might be risking exposure. I had no choice but to retrieve my keys, so with some reluctance I retraced my steps towards the courtyard.

When I stepped fully nude into the view of the other apartments and a public street, a surge of energy raced through my body, centering on my balls. My cock was beginning to stiffen so I quickened my pace. I found my keys where I had left them and hurriedly walked back. The feeling was so euphoric that by the time I had reached the top of my stairs my dick was fully erect. At 35 years old nothing had gotten me that hard that quickly since my teenage years. I was hooked. My mind had already planned the next adventure-one that was to be much more public than this and to occur that night.

I dressed, got into my car and headed for a favorite restaurant of mine. A bolder and more daring plan had taken seed. The restaurant was housed in a three-story office complex built over underground parking in a densely populated part of the city. I drove through the upper level of parking, noting the few cars left in the garage and began stripping off my clothes. By the time I reached the lower level I was completely nude-not so daring except for the fact that my convertible top was down. The lower level had a single car parked near the elevator-a late night worker or maybe a diner who had stayed at the restaurant until after closing. I parked near the stairwell, stashed the keys under the front seat and got out. There I stood in a public parking garage completely nude. I walked around the garage for a few minutes enjoying each step the farther away I strayed from the safety net of my car. Wanting to heighten the experience of nudity in a public place, I headed for the elevator.

I had never ridden the elevator in this garage, as I usually park near the stairwell that leads to the restaurant's front door, so I was unsure to where it led on the upper floors. Without assessing the risks, I pushed the "up" button and boarded the elevator completely naked. The doors closed and I pressed Ll. As the elevator rose I couldn't believe what I had done. I was riding totally nude in a public elevator. When the doors opened where would I be? In the building's public courtyard? In the glass vestibule that faces a busy street? In the lobby of a private company? And what if I couldn't get back down? Overwhelmed, I quickly punched the Pl button and breathed a sigh of relief as the elevator came to rest on the upper garage level.

As the doors opened I stepped out into the garage with cock and balls totally exposed, feeling a surge of excitement I had never felt before. I pretended I was leaving my office for the evening and that being nude was an eccentricity my coworkers were used to. I walked towards the few cars left in the garage as if one was mine, reminding myself I needed to go by the cleaners. I enjoyed the way my nipples had hardened and, as my fantasy continued, the thrill began to have its impact on my freely swinging dick. It began to react, as it had before, but this time at a faster pace. Instead of trying to hide my erection I reveled in the view of my penis standing 180 degrees opposite its usual position. I walked slowly among the parked cars-far away from my car and my clothes.

I decided to take the stairwell back down to the lower level where I had parked my car, knowing full well that this was the route many people used to access the popular gay restaurant above. I lingered by the door, half wanting to hear the voices of exiting diners who might catch me standing in the parking garage completely nude and with a raging hard-on. The patrons of my favorite restaurant include many of Dallas' sexiest gay men and my dick got harder as I fantasized about exposing my naked body to some random man, tipsy from an evening of strong margaritas.

A few moments passed and I slipped into the stairwell and walked downstairs with my cock slapping against my stomach at each step. I swung open the door to the lower level where I had parked my car. As I boldly walked the last few paces to clothing and coverage, I caught sight of the exiting taillights of the car that had earlier been parked by the elevator. I had been walking around in the nude for only seven or eight minutes. At some point, the owner of that car had come down to the garage via either the elevator or the stairwell I had just exited. Had he seen me? A jolt of excitement raced through my groin as I realized I could have easily boarded the elevator or stepped into the stairwell completely nude, only to encounter a fully dressed man. Although it had been an outstanding adventure, I wanted more, and the contrast of my naked body to the clothed bodies of other men began to entice me. Where could I go to fulfill the night's most daring adventure?

I pulled on my underwear and shorts leaving my T-shirt on the floorboard. Still hard from excitement, the head and top half of my cock lay completely exposed against my stomach as I exited the garage accelerating towards my next stop. Thoughts of walking nude into a convenience store and casually buying a bottle of water or strolling naked into the post office to mail my bills tempted me.

Driving back towards my apartment I passed a small gay bar, well known for its patrons' lewd conduct. By now it was pushing 1:30 a.m. but several cars still remained in the lot. My final opportunity for public nudity was beckoning me so I pulled into the parking lot and found a spot behind the bar. I threw on my T-shirt but decided to remove my underwear because earlier experiences had taught me that I could get out of my clothes and achieve nudity much more quickly without the barrier of briefs. Conversely, should I run into trouble I could redress in less than half the time.

I entered the establishment and made my way to the counter where I ordered a shot. Any flirtation with public nudity in the past was only successful if I had had a few drinks to take the edge off. Though my first two adventures of the night were achieved in a totally sober state, what I was about to do next would require me to be completely uninhibited.

The bar's clientele included a dozen patrons being served by two bartenders. With the exception of the employees, everyone seemed drunk. As I felt my inhibitions recede, I considered how I might achieve my fantasy. I decided I would order another shot and simply strip down until I was standing in the bar completely nude. At that point I would drink my shot and wait for the crowd's reactions. Maybe I would throw a game of darts with my dick exposed or walk over to study the contents of the jukebox with my bare ass facing the bar. It didn't matter what I did, as long as I could do it naked and in the presence of completely dressed men.

My second shot arrived but as I reached for my zipper I chickened out. I took my drink and walked out onto the smoking patio feeling defeated. I couldn't believe I had gotten so close but was unable to reach the third tier of my naked fantasy. I stayed on the patio alone for a couple of minutes and decided my ultimate naked adventure would have to wait until another time.

As I entered the room I approached a trio of cute, professional guys who were sitting at the bar. They looked as though they had gone to happy hour after work and hadn't yet called it quits. One of them smiled and spoke to me as I passed, so I stopped and struck up a conversation with him. Within a few minutes my second shot had taken affect and I ended up staying for last call. The guy's name was Joe and he talked to me as if we had met before, although I know we hadn't. As 2:00 a.m.

passed, Joe had introduced me to his two friends, one of whom knew the bar's owner. Joe's friend told us we could stay and finish our drinks while the bartenders closed out their registers.

In the now mostly empty bar my newfound friends, who had been complimenting me since our introductions, began touching my chest and back. At some point Joe lifted my T-shirt to run his hands across my chest and stomach and commented that he could see by the absence of a waistband that I wasn't wearing underwear. He pulled my shorts away from my stomach, peered in at my dick and commented to his friends that he liked uncut men. He invited them to take a peek and undid the top button of my shorts so his friends could get a better view. My zipper began inching its way down.

As he let go of my shorts they slipped down past my hip bones revealing about an inch of pubic hair and the crack of my ass. One of the three began gently tugging at the back of my pants, which forced them down until the base of my dick was exposed. Joe recognized that my shorts were perilously close to falling completely off so he reached down and released the last few centimeters of zipper that stood between my coverage and public nudity. In an instant my shorts dropped to the floor. I kicked them to the side and without hesitation raised my arms above my head as they tugged my T-shirt off. My wildest fantasy was coming true!

I stood totally nude with Joe and his friends while two other patrons moved in closer for a better look. The bartenders stopped their cleanup and stood grinning at what was transpiring. Everyone watched as I finished my drink and made small talk with the guys standing near me. I walked over to the jukebox and leaned on the glass pretending to check out the music selections, just so everyone could get a good look at my ass. My cock began to swell with excitement as the reality of what I was doing began to sink in. Moments later, I walked back to my little audience with the most intense erection of the evening. I was standing naked with an enormous hard-on as completely clothed strangers ogled my crotch and butt.

Since the bar had officially closed, no one stopped me from fulfilling my adventure. In fact, I stayed nude for the next 10 minutes as we played a game of pool, until the bartenders told us we needed to leave. As the small crowd and I made our way to the back exit, I could sense the question on everyone's mind-is he going to walk outside naked? One of the bartenders unlocked and opened the door. Without hesitation I waved good-bye to my audience and stepped out into the parking lot carrying my shorts and shirt instead of wearing them.

My car was parked in a space behind the bar, which was mostly shielded from the road by the building and a high fence. I walked slowly towards my car and as an encore for my night's performance, I took a very long time to put my car's manual convertible top back up-all while completely nude and to the enjoyment of the group watching from the bar's back door. As I pulled out of the lot, I gave Joe a wink and tossed him my briefs.

Back in my apartment I began documenting my adventure, feeling as though I'd been through an initiation into a private club known only by the readers of Naked Magazine. I recalled the clothes I had put into the washer earlier that evening and realized they needed to be dried. "Should I put on clothes?" I wondered as I opened the back door.

"Nah."

Kevin M., Dallas, Texas

More Titles at:
www.GoodBoner.com

A Boner Book

More Titles at:
www.GoodBoner.com